I0835242

Merie Vision Publishing, LLC
www.merievisionpublishing.com

Copyright © 2026 by Tarnisha Harper-Phillips

ISBN: 978-1-961213-29-6

Library of Congress Control Number on record

All rights reserved. No part of this book may be reproduced in any form either by electronic or mechanical means, including information storage and retrieval systems, without written permission from the publisher, except by a reviewer who may quote brief images in a review.

Book Design and Editing by Merie Vision Publishing

First Print Edition March 2026

The Book Of Sadie:

Book One Of The Ancestors Series

Tarnisha Harper-Phillips

Dedication

To my mother,

who showed me what it means to endure, to serve, and to rise each day with purpose. Even at seventy-one, you gave your strength to caring for others, never asking for rest. You left this world quietly, just as you lived, doing your duty and showing up.

Your life, your labor, and your love did not end with you. They walk with me. They write through me.

This book is for you, and for all the ancestors whose sacrifices are never forgotten, whose spirits remain present, guiding us forward.

To my husband,

the greatest storyteller I know. You guided me when I doubted, reminded me of the power of words, and helped me find my way back to the story when I felt lost. Your voice, your wisdom, and your belief in me are woven into these pages more than you know.

To my children,

may this book help you understand the meaning of legacy, that you come from strength, sacrifice, and purpose. May it remind you that your dreams matter, that they are worth pursuing, and that you are meant to fulfill them fully and without fear.

Everything here is written with love, for where we have been, and for all that you will become.

PRELUDE

The night air blew a cold, crisp breeze into the open attic window that sent prickles down the back of Sadie's neck. Although a little disoriented, she was awakened by an unsettling feeling. A motionless image stood before her and put a look of fear on her face, leaving the room bleak from the sight. Covering her eyes with the pillow, she began to beg, "Please let this image go away!"

She pleaded and hoped that it was just a shadow of an object from the moonlight that shone brightly from the window, but she knew it wasn't. Then, Sadie felt it walking towards her.

She *knew* it wasn't her imagination.

She *knew* it was real.

She *knew* who it was that had appeared before her.

She also *knew* that this person would appear again.

Even though she loved this person unconditionally, she was deathly afraid. It was a scary, but loving afraid.

Unlike the rest that came to her, it didn't speak a word, but she knew everything that she was faced with doing and the mission it had for her to complete. Her legs shivered as she removed the covers from the twin bed that she was sleeping on. Suddenly, the vision of the object opened its arms and waited for an embrace.

The smell coming from the vision lingered through the air, blowing from the opened window. It was a scent she would never forget. She began walking slowly towards it with her arms open. The embrace was comforted by the softness of a belly that was only in her reach. As Sadie began to hug this image, a long but frightened sigh of relief came over her as her eyes filled with tears. Hugging her tightly yet in a loving manner, Sadie whispered, "Hey, Grandma."

She held me close, but did not reveal her face. The embrace was all she needed. The stroke of her hand caressed Sadie's back as she began to listen to the words coming from her body. Oddly enough, she didn't speak from her mouth - the words came from her belly. Sadie listened carefully to her thoughts and was attuned with her through her touch. As Sadie's ears pressed firmly against her, the words traveled from her stomach to her ears.

"Sadie, there is still work that needs to be done before my journey is complete in order for me to be at ease and pass through the internal world. I must fulfill my duty through you. I sacrificed my life for my children and their children without completing what I was called to do. Now, I need you to help me complete the task. The mission may seem hard, but if you just follow the plan, I will guide and protect you by all costs."

The images always came when Sadie was at peace. No matter what home they moved into, she always seemed to get the attic. In a house filled with kids and adults, Sadie always ended up with her own room in the attic. She preferred this because she was protected and chosen to do the task of her ancestors. She carried a calling. A calling where secrets were shared to her from those whom she never even met, but the mission had to be done.

It was her duty!

Do you know that we are here for a purpose - a task that needs to be fulfilled? Our Ancestors had everything designed for us. In the equal spirit of our grandmothers meeting up and organizing at the church, in the living rooms, in kitchens, or in ancient healing circles. May we, too, gather our hearts, minds, and spiritual gifts in service to our humanity.

Chapter One
The Doll

Sadie was small for her age - a narrow frame, dark, beautiful skin that glowed bronze in the sunlight, and eyes too deep for a child. People often said she had *"an old soul,"* though she never quite understood what that meant. She was quiet but watchful. She always noticed things others overlooked, such as the sway of the trees when the wind shifted or the way voices echoed differently in her grandmother's house after sundown.

She lived with her grandmother, *Verna Harper*, in a small, timeworn home tucked at the end of a street where every porch had its own story. The house carried the scent of starch, lemon polish, and lilacs - a smell that never seemed to fade, no matter the season. She lived with her because her mother was away for work - at least that's what everyone told her. Letters came sometimes folded neatly and signed with hearts, but never phone calls or visits. Sadie missed her, though she didn't say it much. She just held on to Verna's words,

"Your mama's working to make things better. You just keep her in your prayers."

And that she did. Every night, before she closed her eyes, she whispered,

"Bring Mama home safe."

Sadie daydreamed more than most. Her mind was always somewhere between the clouds and the stories she made up in her head. She loved listening to older people talk, especially Verna's friends who visited for coffee and long afternoons of gossip. They laughed loudly, talked softly, and told stories about "the old ways" - things Sadie didn't always understand but felt in her bones. Kids her age teased her. They would say she was strange, that she "talked like a teacher" or "acted grown," but Sadie didn't mind. She liked the company of old souls. They made her feel seen.

Her eighth birthday came on a humid August afternoon. The kind of day when the air sticks to your skin and the sky feels too close. Balloons swayed lazily from the porch railings. Verna baked a lopsided but sweet vanilla cake, while neighborhood kids crowded the kitchen, laughing and shouting. Sadie tried to smile, but her heart felt heavy each time she looked at the empty chair at the table - the one where her mother should have been. Verna noticed. She came over and brushed a curl from Sadie's forehead.

"Don't you start crying on your birthday," she said gently. "Your aunt's bringing you something special. You'll see."

Moments later, a soft knock echoed through the house. Aunt Carol stepped inside, her floral dress swaying, her face glowing in the warm light. She carried a box wrapped in paper that shimmered like pearls.

"There's my birthday girl," she said, her voice warm like honey.

Sadie ran to her and hugged her tightly. Carol's arms smelled like rose oil and home.

"Happy eighth birthday, baby," she said. "Eight is special, you know that?"

Sadie tilted her head. "Why?"

Carol smiled and took her hand, leading her out to the porch, away from the noise of the other children.

"Because eight means you're growing into your light. It's the year your spirit starts to remember who you are." Sadie blinked, unsure what that meant. Carol squeezed her small hand. "When your parents had you, all they ever wanted was to keep you safe. They asked us to make sure we took care of you, and that's what we're doing. You're surrounded by love, even when it feels quiet."

Sadie's eyes filled with tears. "But I miss Mama."

"I know," Carol whispered, kneeling to meet her eyes. "She misses you too. Sometimes love has to work from far away, but it's still love, baby. It never stops being that."

Sadie nodded, her bottom lip trembling. "Why does it hurt, then?"

Carol smiled sadly. "Because real love always comes with a little ache." She brushed a tear from Sadie's cheek. "Here," she said, handing her the box. "Maybe this will make it feel a little better."

Sadie sat cross-legged on the porch steps, the cicadas humming in the distance as she untied the twine. Inside was a polished wooden box with carvings so delicate they almost shimmered. The hinges creaked as she opened it. Inside lay a doll - old, delicate, and unlike anything she'd ever seen. Her dress was made of lace, the color of faded ivory, stitched with tiny pearls along the sleeves. Her shoes were worn smooth, her hands folded neatly in her lap, but what stopped Sadie cold were her eyes - diamond-like stones, clear and glittering, catching the sunlight as if they held stars inside them.

Sadie gasped. "She's beautiful."

Carol nodded softly. "She's been in our family a long time. Her name..." she paused, her eyes flicking toward the living room where Verna was watching, "...her name doesn't matter right now. What matters is that she'll keep you company when you miss your mama. This doll has been passed through generations of strong women. She listens, and she remembers." Sadie grinned wide, hugging the doll close.

Behind her, a few of the children giggled.

"That's old!" one said.

"Looks creepy," another whispered.

Sadie frowned. "She's not creepy - she's special."

Aunt Carol put an arm around her shoulder. "That's right, baby. Sometimes things that look different just carry more stories."

Verna appeared in the doorway, her face tight. "Alright now," she said, her voice too calm. "Time for cake."

Sadie didn't notice the way her grandmother's eyes lingered on the doll or how she whispered something under her breath as the candlelight flickered.

That night, after the laughter faded and the balloons sagged, Sadie sat in her bed, cradling the doll. The moonlight slipped through her curtains, landing on its glassy, diamond eyes.

"Thank you for being my gift," she whispered. "I'll take care of you."

Outside, the wind stirred softly, brushing against the window. The doll's eyes caught the light again - a faint, shimmering flicker. Sadie smiled and drifted to sleep, the doll beside her pillow, its hands still folded, its head turned ever so slightly toward her. Verna peeked in before bed. For a long time, she just stood there watching the child sleep, her gaze lingering on the doll.

"Lord," she whispered, voice trembling, "not again."

Then she closed the door, sealing the room in quiet.

Under the soft hum of the night, the house sighed as if it, too, remembered.

Chapter Two
Whispers in Verna's House

Sadie had her little routines, the kind that made her feel safe when the world around her seemed too quiet. Every night before bed, she placed her belongings neatly into the small chest at the foot of her bed - her favorite storybook, the comb Aunt Carol gave her, the silver bracelet Grandma Verna said once belonged to her mother, and now, her doll with the diamond eyes. That chest was her secret world, her way of ending the day in order. She would open it, touch each item, whisper a *thank-you* under her breath, and then close it softly before saying her prayers. Tonight felt different, though. The air carried the faint scent of the cake from earlier and the lavender oil Verna dabbed on her pillows. The house hummed with the kind of stillness that made Sadie aware of every sound - the soft ticking of the clock in the hallway, the creak of the floor near the bathroom, and the sigh of the summer wind against the curtains.

She took her evening bath like always. The water was warm, the kind that made her sleepy. She liked watching the soap bubbles swirl, forming little patterns that looked like faces for a second before fading away. Sometimes she imagined they were trying to speak to her.

When she stepped out and wrapped herself in a towel, she caught her reflection in the fogged-up mirror. Her curls were damp, her skin glowing from the steam. For a moment, she smiled at herself - a shy, proud smile - because even though she was just eight, she *felt* older tonight.

On her bed, she admired all of her birthday gifts again - the coloring book from Miss Jenkins down the street, the necklace from her cousin, the blue ribbons, and the little bottle of perfume shaped like a heart. Each one made her feel seen, remembered. Then, she picked up the nightgown her grandmother gave her. It was a soft cotton and the color of deep purple twilight. It was her favorite. The fabric was smooth against her skin. The color reminding her of quiet evenings and her grandmother's soft humming in the kitchen. She held it up in front of the mirror, admiring how it shimmered in the light. The lace around the collar was delicate, hand-stitched. Verna had told her it once belonged to someone "special," though she hadn't said who. Sadie didn't ask. She just pressed the nightgown to her face and inhaled the faint scent of lilac and cedar.

"I'm going to wear this forever," she whispered to her reflection, grinning at her own silliness.

As she slipped it over her head, she felt comforted as if the fabric itself was holding her close. She brushed her hair, crawled into bed, and reached for her book, *The Little Prince*, a story she loved though she didn't always understand it. She liked how the boy in the story kept asking grown-ups questions they couldn't answer. It made her feel less strange for doing the same.

Her doll sat at the edge of the nightstand, facing her. The moonlight from the window caught its eyes, and for a moment, it looked almost awake.

"Goodnight," she said softly, half-laughing. "You don't have to watch me sleep, you know."

The doll, of course, didn't respond, but something in the room changed. Just a feeling, like the air holding its breath. Sadie pulled the covers up to her chin and turned on her side. She listened to the house – the pipes sighing, the wind pressing against the windows, the slow, rhythmic creak of Verna's rocking chair downstairs.

Her eyelids grew heavy, but just before sleep found her, she thought she heard it – a faint hum, like a song she almost recognized but couldn't quite place. She smiled drowsily.

"Grandma," she murmured, half-asleep. "You always hum that song..."

But the voice wasn't Grandma Verna's.

It was softer.

Younger.

From the corner of the room, the doll's diamond eyes caught the moonlight again. This time, flickering twice, like a heartbeat. The humming came again, soft as breath. It floated through the room, rising and falling like the sound of someone pacing slowly, singing to themselves. Sadie's eyes fluttered open. The moonlight had shifted across her walls, tracing silver lines along the furniture. The sound grew clearer. Not a tune she knew, but a lullaby that felt strangely familiar, like something she'd heard once long ago and forgotten. She sat up, clutching her blanket. The doll was still where she'd left it, though its head seemed slightly turned, the diamond eyes fixed toward the doorway.

"Grandma?" she whispered.

No answer.

Sadie slid out of bed, her bare feet brushing against the cool wooden floor. The humming continued, drifting down the hallway. It was a woman's voice, tender, calm, but carrying a sadness that made her chest ache. She crept toward the door, careful not to wake the floorboards. Her small fingers curled around the frame as she peered into the hall. It was empty, the air heavy and still, but the sound didn't stop. It seemed to be coming from *downstairs.*

Sadie tiptoed down the steps, each one groaning softly beneath her. The house smelled faintly of burnt wax and soap. A single lamp glowed from the living room, casting long shadows against the walls.

"Grandma?"

Still nothing.

She followed the sound to the kitchen. The door was cracked open, and from inside came the faint rhythm of humming now mixed with the sound of running water. Sadie pushed the door open. The sink was dripping slowly. The window curtains shifted, though the air was still. On the counter sat a candle, burned almost to its base. Its flame bent sideways, stretching toward the corner of the room.

There, near the pantry, stood a shape.

A woman's figure, her back turned, her head bowed slightly as she hummed that same strange tune. Her dress shimmered faintly in the dim light - pale, old-fashioned, almost see-through.

Sadie's voice trembled. "Grandma?"

The humming stopped.

The figure stilled.

When the woman turned, the light flickered. Sadie saw nothing but a blur of dark hair and soft eyes - eyes that looked almost *like hers.*

The candle went out.

Sadie!" Her grandmother's voice cracked the silence. Verna appeared in the doorway, her robe pulled tight around her. "What you doin' up, child?"

Sadie turned, heart racing. "I heard you humming, Grandma. I thought—"

Verna glanced around the kitchen, her eyes narrowing. The candle was still smoking. "You thought what?"

Sadie looked toward the pantry again. The corner was empty now. Only the faint scent of lilacs lingered in the air.

"Nothing," she whispered. "I just thought you were downstairs."

Verna exhaled slowly, her eyes darting toward the pantry one last time. "You shouldn't be wandering around this late. Go on back to bed."

Sadie hesitated. "Did you hear it, Grandma?"

Verna's face hardened, but her voice softened. "It's an old house, baby. Houses talk when they get tired. Now go on."

Sadie nodded and climbed the stairs, glancing back only once. Verna stood perfectly still in the kitchen doorway, staring at the spot where the candle had been. Her hand trembled slightly as she reached for it, running her thumb across the melted wax. She whispered something under her breath - a name, perhaps - before blowing out the last wisp of smoke.

Upstairs, Sadie crawled back into bed. The doll lay beside her chest, its eyes catching the faint glow from the hallway.

She whispered, "Who were you singing to?"

The wind pressed softly against the windowpane, like a breath.

Downstairs, Verna stayed awake long after the house went quiet again. She sat in her chair by the window, rocking slowly, her gaze lost in the darkness. She didn't need to look at the old photo album in the drawer to know what she'd seen. She already knew the scent, the song, the shimmer in the air.

It was *her mother's hum.*

The one she hadn't heard since the night Thema, her mother, died.

The knowing came over her like a chill.

The spirit hadn't just returned.

It had *found its way to Sadie.*

Chapter Three

The Note Under the Pillow

The smell of breakfast drifted through the air. It smelled of fried potatoes, butter, and something sweet, maybe cornbread or warm biscuits. It was the kind of smell that usually made Sadie smile, but this morning it took her a moment to remember where she was. Her eyes fluttered open slowly, heavy with sleep. The light poured through her curtains in thin ribbons, slicing across her blanket. For a moment, she just lay there, listening to the quiet hum of the house and the faint clatter of dishes downstairs. Then she stretched her small hands, brushing across her pillow, and felt something gritty. She frowned, sitting up, still half-dreaming. Tiny specks of dark soil clung to the white fabric, sprinkled like crumbs. As she lifted her pillow, a few fell to the floor, landing softly on the wooden boards.

"Where'd that come from?" she mumbled to herself, rubbing her eyes.

The sight made her uneasy. She didn't remember bringing anything dirty to bed, and she'd taken her bath, folded her clothes neatly, just like always. She slipped one foot out of bed, then the other, searching under the frame for her slippers. They were tucked just where she left them, soft and pink and slightly worn. She slid them on and stood, brushing sleep from her eyes. Her gaze caught on the mirror across the room.

The morning light was soft, golden, spilling across her nightgown. It was Grandma Verna's gift. She walked toward the mirror slowly, her reflection still sleepy, curls tousled, eyes puffy from the night. When she reached the dresser, she lifted her face towel to wipe her cheeks, but paused. The **doll** sat there, right beside the mirror, perfectly upright. Sadie's breath hitched. She was sure... *sure...* she'd left it on her chest the night before, folded gently under her book. Now it sat facing her reflection, hands in its lap, head slightly tilted.

"Grandma?" she called, her voice cracking in the quiet room.

No answer. Only the faint scrape of a chair from the kitchen below. She turned back to the doll. The sunlight made its diamond eyes glimmer, tiny sparks of light dancing across the mirror's surface. For a moment, it looked almost alive. A chill crawled up her arms. She stepped closer, studying its face. The faint crack near its temple, the perfectly painted lips, *everything.*

Her voice trembled. "How'd you get over here?"

She reached out slowly, but stopped before touching it. Something about those eyes made her hesitate. It wasn't out of fear, exactly, but out of a strange respect, like she was standing too close to something sacred. Downstairs, Grandma Verna called, "Breakfast's ready, baby!"

Sadie blinked, shaking off the strange feeling. She took one last glance in the mirror, at her reflection, the doll, and the dirt on the pillow. Then, she turned toward the hallway. The morning air was warmer now and the smell of food wrapped around her like comfort. The creak of floorboards beneath her feet echoed softly as she made her way down the stairs.

"Morning, Grandma," she said, trying to sound cheerful.

Grandma Verna looked up from the stove, her eyes tired but kind. "Morning, baby. Sleep good?"

Sadie hesitated. "I think so. I had a weird dream, though."

Grandma Verna flipped the potatoes, her back turned. "Dreams are just the mind cleaning itself out. Eat your breakfast before it gets cold."

Sadie sat at the table, her hands folded neatly in her lap. The plate was full with eggs, toast, and sausage, everything warm and perfect, but she wasn't hungry. The memory of the dirt clinging to her pillow wouldn't leave her. She looked toward the hallway that led back to her room. The house was quiet again - too quiet. Then she remembered.

The humming.

The shape in the kitchen.

The flicker of the candlelight.

Her spoon clinked against the plate as her hand trembled. "Grandma," she said softly, "do you ever hear... singing at night?"

Grandma Verna froze mid-motion. The spatula hovered above the pan. She turned slowly. "What kind of singing?"

Sadie's voice dropped to a whisper. "Like a lady's voice. Not loud. Just... there."

Grandma Verna stared at her for a long time before answering. Her face was calm, but her eyes gave her away. They looked scared, the way eyes do when old memories come knocking.

"Probably just the wind," Grandma Verna said. "That old house hums sometimes. Been doin' it since before you were born."

Sadie nodded, though she didn't believe her. She took another small bite, staring down at her food. When she looked up again, she caught her grandmother watching her/ It wasn't in the way adults watch children, but in the way people study something they can't quite explain.

Grandma Verna turned away quickly, wiping her hands on a towel. "Eat up, now. You got a long day ahead."

Later that morning, when Sadie went back upstairs, her bed was neatly made, except for one thing. On her pillow lay a **folded piece of paper**. The edges were yellowed, soft, and faintly torn. Her heart pounded. She unfolded it slowly. In the center, written in small, delicate handwriting, were the words:

"When the wind speaks your name... listen."

Sadie blinked, her mouth falling open. The paper trembled in her hands. It wasn't her handwriting, but it was signed with her name.

Sadie.

Sadie sat on the edge of her bed, staring at the note. The handwriting looked soft - looped letters, careful, almost like the way her grandmother wrote grocery lists, but thinner, lighter... older. She traced her name at the bottom, whispering it under her breath.

"Sadie."

It didn't feel like she'd written it. It felt like the house had. Her fingers brushed the edge of the paper. It smelled faintly of something earthy. It wasn't ink, nor dust, but soil. The same smell that clung to her pillow that morning. She turned slowly toward the mirror. The doll still sat there, its diamond eyes catching the afternoon light. One spark flashed across its face, like a wink. Sadie frowned. "You didn't do this, did you?" she whispered, half teasing, half scared.

Of course, there was no answer, but the air shifted again. A small thing, like the breath of wind moving through a closed room. She noticed something else on the floor beside the dresser. Tiny crumbs of dirt trailed from the bed to the mirror, faint but clear, like a line someone had walked through barefoot. She knelt down, brushing her fingers across the floorboards. The dirt was cool, moist, and when she lifted her hand, a small speck clung to her skin... black as ash.

Her chest tightened.

There hadn't been any dirt in the room the night before. She followed the faint trail across the floor, past her chest, and toward the window. The curtain swayed gently, though the window was still closed. Outside, the yard lay silent.

The trees still, the world unmoving.

Sadie pressed her hand against the glass, peering out. There, at the far edge of the yard near the old oak, something caught her eye - a patch of ground darker than the rest, as though it had been freshly disturbed. A shadow flickered across it, but left as soon as it appeared. Sadie stepped back quickly, heart hammering. The room suddenly felt colder, tighter. Her eyes darted toward the doll again. It sat perfectly still with it's hands folded, face serene. But somehow, she couldn't shake the feeling that the doll was listening.

Sadie!" Verna's voice floated up from downstairs. "Come help me hang these sheets before the sun goes down!"

Sadie quickly folded the note and tucked it under her pillow again. She didn't know why she hid it but she knew that she needed to. Before she left the room, she glanced back one last time. The sunlight had shifted again, landing directly on the doll's eyes. For a moment, the room shimmered. It was faint, golden, and like dust caught midair. Then, the light dimmed.

Sadie blinked, unsure if she'd imagined it. She took a slow breath and whispered,

"When the wind speaks your name... listen."

The words felt strange leaving her mouth, but they settled somewhere deep inside her like a key turning in a lock she didn't know existed. Before her thought took over, she decided to head downstairs and see what everyone else was doing. She found Grandma Verna on the back porch, folding white sheets that smelled like sunshine and soap. The air was warm, cicadas buzzing faintly in the trees.

Grandma Verna smiled when she saw her. "You moving kinda slow today, baby. You feeling all right?"

Sadie nodded. "Just sleepy, I guess."

"You had a big day yesterday. Turning eight ain't no small thing," Verna said, shaking out a sheet. "You're stepping into your light now."

Sadie smiled faintly. "Aunt Carol said the same thing."

"Smart woman," Verna said, clipping the sheet to the line. "Now hand me that one."

As Sadie passed her another, her gaze drifted toward the far corner of the yard where the ground looked darker. She thought about the dirt on her pillow, the note, the whisper in the night. For a second, she opened her mouth to say something, but Grandma Verna's humming filled the silence. It was soft, low, and the same tune as before. It wrapped around Sadie like a spell, familiar yet haunting. She swallowed her words and kept folding, but she couldn't stop her eyes from wandering back to that dark patch of earth. Somewhere deep down, something told her, whatever happened last night hadn't stayed there.

It had followed her into the morning.

Chapter Four

The Song in the Walls

Sunday morning came with sunlight spilling through the stained-glass windows of the small church on the corner of Ashland and Maple. The air smelled of perfume, pressed linen, and old wood warmed by years of prayer. Every bench creaked under the weight of hats, Bibles, and softly whispered "Amens." Sadie stood near the front of the sanctuary, hands clasped tightly in front of her. Her heart thudded against her chest - not fast, but heavy, the way it does when something inside wants to run and hide.

She looked down at herself, trying to find calm in the small details of what she wore.

Her white dress, the one Grandma Verna ironed the night before, fell just below her knees, crisp with tiny pleats that fluttered when she moved. The lace collar tickled her neck, and she tried not to fidget with it too much. Her patent leather shoes gleamed under the church lights, polished so bright she could almost see her reflection in them. They pinched a little at the heel, but she didn't dare complain. Verna had said, *"Every lady needs a little shine on Sunday."*

Her stockings were a size too big, sliding down to her arches no matter how tightly she pulled them up that morning. She could feel the extra fabric bunching under her feet, rubbing against her shoes. She shifted from one foot to the other, trying to fix them without drawing attention. The floorboards squeaked beneath her as she did, their old rhythm echoing like a sigh from the building itself. The church was filled with familiar faces. As always, Deacon Harris was wiping his brow, Sister May was fanning herself with the program, and the children's choir lined neatly in front of the pulpit, waiting their turn.

Sadie's turn.

Her stomach twisted. Her name was next on the list, written neatly on the choir schedule:

Solo - Sadie Harper.

The organ hummed low, like a heartbeat under the surface of the air. Sister Jenkins, the choir director, gave her a gentle nod from across the aisle.

"Ready, baby?" she mouthed.

Sadie tried to smile, but her lips felt stiff. She looked down again, staring at her shoes, her stockings, the edge of her white hem, just searching for something, *anything*, to hold onto.

Her palms were slick with sweat. The hymnbook trembled slightly in her grip. That's when she lifted her eyes. Across the sea of faces, near the third pew, she found her grandmother. Verna sat with her hands folded on her lap, her Sunday hat tilted just right, her scarf, the pale blue one, draped loosely around her shoulders. She didn't say a word, didn't gesture or nod. She just smiled.

That smile was enough.

It was calm, knowing, full of quiet pride. It carried every lesson, every bedtime story, every whispered prayer. It told Sadie without words:

You're safe. You're loved. Sing, baby.

Sadie took a deep breath. Her shoulders relaxed. The tremor in her hands stilled. Sister Jenkins lifted her hand to cue the pianist, and the first soft notes floated into the room. The melody was familiar. It was the hymn Grandma Verna always hummed while cooking or folding laundry.

Sadie stepped forward, her patent leather shoes clicking against the wood, her small frame now standing in front of the pulpit. The light from the stained glass touched her face, painting her cheeks in soft reds and golds. She opened her mouth to sing. The first note came out small, uncertain, but then she saw Verna again - that same steady smile, eyes glistening - and Sadie's voice found its place.

She sang.

Her voice rose, pure and trembling, filling the old church with something fragile and beautiful. People turned in their seats. Even the babies quieted. For a moment, it felt like the sound didn't belong to her alone. It felt shared as if someone else was singing through her, weaving their voice into hers. When the last note faded, silence lingered. Then the congregation erupted into applause.

"Sing, baby!" someone shouted from the back.

Sadie's face flushed with pride and surprise. She smiled shyly, eyes drifting back to Grandma Verna who wiped a tear from her cheek and mouthed, "That's my girl."

As Sadie stepped down from the choir risers, something caught her ear.

A faint hum.

The same melody, echoing, but not from the church band.

It came from behind her.

From somewhere *near the walls.*

The church service carried on around her, the murmurs of praise, the rustle of hymnbooks, the clapping that still echoed long after she sat back down. Sadie could barely hear it. She kept glancing toward the far corner of the sanctuary near the old wooden walls, where the faint humming had come from. It was almost too soft to be real, a whisper behind the music. Yet something about it made her skin prickle.

She sat quietly beside Grandma Verna, trying to listen without drawing attention. Every time she thought it had stopped, the sound returned, low, sweet, and somehow familiar. The same tune she had just sung. Her fingers twisted in her lap. She leaned close to her grandmother. "Grandma," she whispered, "do you hear that?"

Verna turned, her smile gentle but her eyes cautious. "Hear what, baby?"

"The song. Somebody's still humming it."

Verna listened for a moment, then shook her head. "Ain't nobody humming. You must still have the sound stuck in your head."

Sadie nodded, though she wasn't convinced. The sound was still there, just under the surface, like a secret the walls refused to keep quiet.

After the service, when the crowd began to file out, Sadie excused herself. "I'm going to the restroom," she told Verna.

"Alright, baby. Don't take too long," Verna said, already distracted by Sister May and the other ladies offering compliments.

Sadie slipped away, her patent leather shoes tapping softly against the worn floors of the hallway that led to the back of the church. The hallway was dimmer, quieter, sunlight seeping through high windows, dust motes floating lazily in the air. The sound followed her there too.

Soft. Rhythmic. Humming.

She paused by the restroom door, her hand hovering over the handle. "Hello?" she called softly.

No answer.

She pushed the door open.

The small restroom smelled faintly of soap and old wood. Two sinks lined the wall, their mirrors cracked slightly at the corners. A single lightbulb flickered overhead, casting slow, uneven shadows that moved when she did. She stepped closer to the mirror and stared at herself, cheeks flushed, eyes wide, hair curling against her forehead. She looked older somehow, or maybe just more aware.

The humming came again.

Not from behind her.

Not from the hall.

From inside the room.

Sadie's breath caught. "Who's there?" Her voice echoed softly off the tiled walls. The air seemed to thicken, heavy and cool, carrying the faint scent of lilacs.

Then, just beneath the flickering light, the mirror began to fog, slowly, like someone was breathing on the other side. Sadie stepped back. "Grandma?" No response.

The fog spread wider, covering her reflection completely. Then, right in the middle of the glass, a small, clear circle appeared, wiped clean from the inside. Through it, a pair of eyes looked back at her.
They weren't hers. They were older, dark, soft, and shimmering like water in moonlight.

Sadie's hand flew to her mouth. She froze, unable to move. The figure behind the glass leaned closer. A faint voice, low and melodic, drifted out, though the lips in the mirror never moved.

"Don't be afraid, little one."

Sadie stumbled backward. "Who are you?"

The light flickered once, twice, then steadied. The figure came into full view. It was a young woman, maybe sixteen, dressed in a pale dress with lace sleeves. Her face was kind, but sad. Her hair was braided down her back, the same way Sadie sometimes wore hers. Around her neck hung a long, worn scarf. The same scarf Sadie had seen in her dream.

The woman's voice was a whisper, echoing like wind through trees. "You have her voice."

"Whose voice?" Sadie asked, trembling.

The woman smiled faintly. "Mine."

The bathroom door burst open. "Sadie!" Grandma Verna's voice filled the room.

Sadie spun around. The mirror cleared instantly, only her reflection staring back. "What are you doin' in here so long?" Verna asked, breathless.

Sadie looked at the mirror again. The fog had vanished. No eyes. No humming. Just her own frightened face staring back. "I... I thought I saw someone," she whispered.

Verna's gaze followed hers to the mirror. She stood very still for a long moment, then crossed herself quietly. "Come on," she said finally, her voice low. "We're goin' home."

As they walked toward the car, Sadie looked back at the church one last time. Through the tall stained glass window, she thought she saw movement, a faint, pale shape near the wall where she had been standing earlier. Though she couldn't hear the hum anymore, she swore she could feel it inside her chest, soft and steady, like a second heartbeat.

Chapter Five

The 3 A.M. Visit

The night came heavy and quiet, the kind that pressed down on the house and made every sound feel louder once it arrived. Rain had passed through earlier, leaving the world damp and shining under the moon. The pavement outside glistened like polished stone, and the scent of wet earth lingered in the air. Crickets sang in long, steady rhythms, filling the dark with their chorus, and somewhere down the block, a dog barked once before falling silent again.

Sadie lay awake in her bed, staring at the ceiling. Shadows from the trees outside swayed gently across the walls, stretching and shrinking as the branches moved with the breeze. Her mind refused to settle. It kept circling back to the church, replaying the moment over and over again.

Her song.

The applause that followed. The mirror. The woman with the soft eyes who had looked at her as if she already knew her.

"You have her voice."

The words had rooted themselves deep inside her, curling around her thoughts until she could not pull free. She told herself it had only been a trick of the light, or maybe a dream that slipped into her waking mind. She tried to believe it had been nothing more than her imagination running wild after a long Sunday. The feeling stayed with her anyway, steady and insistent, like something waiting to be acknowledged.

The doll sat on her dresser, just as it always did. Tonight, Sadie could not bring herself to look directly at it. The moonlight fell across its face at the perfect angle, catching in its crystal eyes and making them glow faintly. She turned away from it and pulled the blanket up to her chin as if the extra layer might quiet her thoughts.

Grandma Verna had checked on her before bed, lingering in the doorway longer than usual. She had not said much. She had only brushed her fingers across Sadie's forehead and whispered,

"Sleep deep, baby."

Her voice had trembled, just enough for Sadie to notice.

At first, sleep came easily. The weight of the night pressed her down into the mattress, and her thoughts finally slowed. Sometime deep in the darkness, a sound began to pull her back.

It was a hum.

Low and soft, carrying the same melody from church.

Sadie blinked, half awake, as silver blue moonlight spilled through the window and washed over her room. The hum grew clearer, closer, as though it were moving through the air itself. It wrapped around her like warmth, familiar and unsettling all at once. She pushed herself up slowly, her heart thudding against her ribs. The clock on her nightstand glowed faintly in the dark.

3:00 A.M.

The same hour when the house always seemed to settle and complain at the same time.

"Grandma Verna?" she called softly.

No answer came.

The hum deepened, filling the room without growing louder. It did not frighten her. It carried something she did not have words for yet, a mix of sadness and love that made her chest ache. Sadie swung her legs out of bed, her bare feet brushing against the cool wooden floor. The boards creaked beneath her weight. She shivered and glanced toward the dresser.

The doll was no longer facing the mirror. It was facing her pillow. Sadie froze. She knew she had not left it that way. The humming shifted, drifting toward the hallway like a gentle pull. Sadie followed, each step careful and slow. The air felt thicker as she moved, charged in a way she could feel against her skin.

She passed Grandma Verna's door. Her grandmother's soft snores rose and fell in a steady rhythm, safe and familiar. Comfort washed over Sadie for just a moment. Then the hum grew stronger again, calling her forward from the living room below. She descended the stairs, her fingers sliding along the cool railing. Moonlight poured through the windows, bathing the house in silver. In the center of the living room, the air shimmered faintly, rippling as if heat were rising from the floor. Then the hum formed words.

"Sadie..." Her name floated through the room, sung so gently it barely sounded like a voice.

Sadie stopped at the foot of the stairs. "Who's there?" she asked.

The shimmer brightened and stretched upward, shaping itself into the outline of a figure. The glow trembled as it took form, soft and unsteady, as if it were learning how to exist in the room. Sadie's breath caught as the figure became clearer. A young woman stood before her, dressed in a pale gown that seemed to glow in the moonlight. Her hair was braided down her back, and her face was half-lit and half-shadowed. It was the same woman from the mirror.

Thema.

Their eyes met. Thema's were deep and kind, filled with a sadness that felt familiar.

"I told you not to be afraid," Thema whispered. Her voice carried the sound of music, wind, and heartbeat all at once.

Sadie wanted to run, but her legs would not move. "Why are you here?" she asked.

Thema glanced toward the stairs before looking back at her. "Because the song found you."

"I don't understand," Sadie said, her voice shaking.

"You will," Thema replied softly. "You were chosen to carry what was silenced."

The air around them shimmered again, and the room filled with the faint scent of lilacs and rain. A creak sounded behind them.

"Sadie?" Grandma Verna's voice came from the stairs, groggy and frightened. "What are you doin' up?"

Sadie turned, and in that instant the light dimmed. Thema's form began to fade, her voice thinning as it melted into the air. "Tell her I remember."

The last thing Sadie saw was the edge of Thema's scarf lifting like smoke before she disappeared.

Grandma Verna rushed down the stairs, her robe tied tight, her eyes wide.

"Sadie! Lord, child, what's wrong?"

Sadie's face had gone pale.

"She was here."

"Who was here?" Grandma Verna asked.

"The lady from the mirror," Sadie whispered. "She said my name. She said she remembers."

Grandma Verna's breath caught. She looked toward the empty space Sadie pointed to, her hands beginning to shake.

"Go on upstairs," she said softly. "Right now."

"But Grandma Verna—"

"Go on."

Sadie obeyed, her feet thudding up the stairs and leaving Grandma Verna alone in the living room. The house fell quiet again, but Grandma Verna could still feel it. The echo of the hum. The pulse of something old and aching that had never truly left. She sank into her chair, pressing her trembling hands together.

"Lord," she whispered into the empty room, "why now?"

A gust of wind swept through the house, though every window was closed. The candle on the table flickered once, then went still.

From somewhere unseen, a woman's voice answered, soft and certain.

"Because it's time."

Chapter Six

Verna's Silence

Morning light crept through the curtains, pale and tired, settling quietly over the house as though it, too, had not rested well. The air felt heavy, unmoving, and the only sound was the wind brushing against the windowpanes in long, restless sighs. Verna sat at the kitchen table with her coffee untouched, her fingers wrapped loosely around the mug as she stared into the steam, waiting for it to shape itself into answers she already knew would not come. Sleep had barely touched her through the night, and each time her eyes closed, she saw the same shimmer of light in the living room. It was that faint but familiar glow that had once terrified her when she was a child and now returned like a memory refusing to stay buried.

The doll sat on the table just as she had found it at dawn, upright in the chair across from her with its hands folded neatly in its lap, as though it had placed them there with intention. Verna had not moved it and could not bring herself to try. The longer she looked at it, the heavier her chest became, as if the years she had worked so hard to lock away were pressing forward all at once. She watched it from across the room as her thoughts drifted through moments she had convinced herself were only stories – things best left unspoken and untouched.

The smell of damp earth reached her then, slow and unmistakable, curling through the room as if carried on unseen breath. It was the same scent that had followed her all her life, wet soil after rain, lilac on the wind, and something older that felt like memory clinging to the air. Her eyes moved toward the counter, where a thin dusting of dirt lay scattered beside the sink. It was not much, just enough to make her heart sink. She did not need to touch it to know where it had come from, because the feeling in her bones had already told her. The ground was moving again, and the ancestors were stirring. Verna closed her eyes and tried to steady her breathing, counting each rise and fall of her chest, but the past came anyway, slow and uninvited.

She was eight years old again, sitting on the edge of her grandmother Bibi's bed while the heavy summer air pressed against the walls and cicadas filled the room like a steady heartbeat. Bibi brushed her hair that night with long, careful strokes, humming the same tune Sadie had sung in church. The melody had always made Verna sleepy because it was soft and low, wrapping around her like the world itself was rocking her in its arms and promising safety it could never truly give.

The knock on the window came suddenly, three soft taps that never changed, no matter how many years passed. Bibi did not flinch. She only stopped humming and whispered, "Don't look, baby," her voice calm in a way that made Verna's stomach twist, but Verna looked anyway. Outside, beyond the glow of the oil lamp, her mother stood in the yard. Thema was young and beautiful, dressed in white, her body still as moonlight, and her face unreadable.

"Grandma," Verna had whispered, her voice trembling despite her effort to be brave, "Mama's outside."

Bibi's hands froze in her hair. "No, baby. That ain't her."

Even then, Verna knew better. She could feel it deep in her chest, a knowing that did not need proof. Thema smiled then, soft and sad, and lifted her hand as if she were trying to wave, as if distance alone stood between them. The wind stirred, scattering dust from the windowsill into the room, and by the time Verna blinked, her mother was gone, leaving only silence behind.

Bibi crossed herself three times and whispered the chant Verna would never forget, her words low and urgent as she called on wind, blood, and the circle of mothers to guard their line. That was the night Verna learned that spirits never truly leave, and that silence, once learned, can be both a shield and a curse.

She opened her eyes and returned to the present, her hand trembling as she set the coffee cup down on the table. Her gaze moved toward the living room where Sadie still slept on the couch, worn out from the night before. The child's face was peaceful now, her small hand curled tightly around Verna's scarf as though it offered safety even in sleep, and the sight tightened something deep in Verna's chest.

"She's too young," Verna whispered to the quiet room, her voice barely more than breath. "Just like I was."

She crossed to the sink and wiped the dirt away with the edge of her dish towel, moving slowly, deliberately, as if rushing might make it worse. Each stroke felt like a prayer passed down through generations of women who had tried to clean away what could not be washed, who had learned to keep moving even when the weight of knowing pressed heavily. When she finished, she stood at the window and stared out into the yard where the oak trees swayed gently, their roots running deeper than memory and deeper than time.

"Why'd you come back now, Mama?" she whispered, her reflection faint in the glass. "You could've stayed resting."

No answer came, only the soft movement of the curtains that sounded like a sigh. Verna reached into her pocket and wrapped her fingers around her rosary beads, the small wooden cross smooth from years of use and worry. She began to pray, her voice low and unsteady as truth pressed its way out of her. "Lord, I know what this is. I know what you're showin' me. But please... don't take her down that road."

Her voice broke as the last of her strength gave way. "Take me instead."

Behind her, the doll's eyes caught the sunlight and sent two small flashes across the floor and up the wall, settling briefly over Verna's heart. She did not see it, but she felt it - the warmth, the pulse, the quiet knowing that did not need words.

Her mother was listening.

The silence Verna had relied on for so long was beginning to break.

Chapter Seven

The Scarf in the Pantry

The day stretched long and golden, sunlight spilling through the kitchen window and painting soft squares on the floor that shifted as the hours passed. The air smelled faintly of rain, though the clouds never came, and the morning settled into a calm that always made Verna hum while she worked. It was the kind of quiet that felt earned, the kind that came after worry but before certainty. Sadie loved mornings like this because they felt like stories. The kind of stories that stayed with you even when no one ever spoke them out loud. She liked the way the house seemed to breathe during moments like this - walls holding warmth, floors remembering footsteps.

"Come on now, baby," Grandma Verna said as she tied her apron, smoothing the fabric down the front the way she always did before starting something important. "We gon' make us a pie today. The kind your mama used to love."

Sadie's face lit up as she slid off the chair. "Apple?"

Grandma Verna smiled, her eyes glimmering with something that reached beyond the kitchen, something that lived just behind her gaze. "You already know."

She pulled a brown paper bag from the counter, its top folded neatly, and set it beside the sink as if it belonged there, as if it had always been waiting for this moment. "Now go wash them apples. Use that old basin by the window. That one always gets the light just right."

Sadie obeyed, standing on her tiptoes to reach the faucet. The apples felt smooth and cool against her skin, heavier than she expected, and she liked the sound they made when they knocked together in the water. The soft hollow thuds echoed in the basin like small heartbeats, steady and patient. She rolled each apple in her hands before setting it aside, watching the droplets slide down and collect at the bottom as sunlight flickered across their skins. The simple task made her feel useful, like she had a place in the rhythm of the morning.

Grandma Verna set out the cutting board and her favorite knife, the one with the wooden handle worn smooth from years of use and care. She ran her thumb along the edge out of habit before nodding toward the apples. "You see these? You gotta slice 'em thin, but not too thin. Let the fruit still have somethin' to say when you bite into it. A pie got feelings just like people do."

Sadie giggled and scrunched her nose. "You talk to the apples, Grandma?"

"Child, I talk to everything that gives me somethin' good," Grandma Verna said with a knowing smile. "That's how you show respect. Things tend to treat you better when you do."

They worked side by side, Grandma Verna slicing with the steady rhythm of someone who had done it more times than she could count, while Sadie carefully laid each piece into the big blue bowl. The sound of the knife against the board filled the kitchen with its own quiet music, sharp and soft all at once. Grandma Verna noticed how carefully Sadie worked, how she took her time lining the slices just right, and something in her chest tightened at the sight. She wondered how many moments like this she had missed before Sadie came to live with her.

How many lessons had gone untaught simply because no one had slowed down long enough.

When all the apples were cut, Grandma Verna sprinkled sugar over them, not too much, just enough to glisten and cling. Cinnamon followed, then nutmeg, and finally a small pinch of salt. The scent bloomed in the air, warm and familiar, wrapping itself around the room like a memory settling in. Grandma Verna closed her eyes for just a moment, letting the smell take her somewhere else, somewhere softer.

"Now this," Grandma Verna said as she reached for a small tin on the shelf, "is what brings it home."

She opened the tin and dipped two fingers inside while Sadie leaned closer, her eyes wide. "What is it?"

"Brown sugar mixed with a little orange zest," Grandma Verna said. "That's the secret. Most folks don't think past cinnamon. One more thing makes it perfect."

She picked up an orange from the counter, its skin bright and dimpled, and sliced a thin round piece before placing it carefully at the bottom of the pie crust. Her movements were slow and intentional, as if she were setting something sacred in place. Verna remembered the first time she had been taught that trick, a quiet voice guiding her hands, telling her not to rush.

Sadie tilted her head. "An orange? Grandma, that don't go in pie!"

Grandma Verna smiled, her eyes twinkling. "That's what most folks think. That slice don't make the pie taste like orange. It just makes everything else taste more like itself. Sweet gets sweeter. Warm gets warmer. That's balance. Life needs that too."

Sadie nodded slowly, the words settling somewhere deeper than baking. "Can I put one in, too?"

"Of course!!"

Sadie placed her slice gently into the dish beside her grandmother's, lining it up just right. Grandma Verna reached over and touched her hand, giving it a soft squeeze that lingered a second longer than necessary. "That's it, baby. Always put a little love in there, too. That's what holds it all together when everything else starts fallin' apart."

As the pie baked, the house filled with its scent, apples softening, butter melting, cinnamon blooming in the heat until it reached every corner. The smell carried safety and home, wrapping itself around the walls and settling into the furniture, into the very bones of the house. Sadie sat at the table watching as Grandma Verna wiped down the counter, her movements slower now and more thoughtful, as if each swipe pulled her deeper into memory. She paused now and then, staring at nothing and listening to something only she could hear.

"Grandma," Sadie said softly, "did my mama help you make pies too?"

She paused, the cloth still in her hand, her eyes drifting toward the window where the light had softened and stretched across the yard. "She did. Used to sit right where you sittin' now, swingin' her legs and askin' the same kind of questions."

Sadie smiled. "Was she good at it?"

Grandma Verna chuckled, the sound gentle and worn. "She was better at eatin' it than makin' it. She tried though. Burned a crust or two along the way. When she got older, she learned. That's how it goes, baby. We all learn from the hands that fed us."

Sadie rested her chin in her hands, turning that over in her mind. The smell from the oven made her feel warm inside, like she was part of something that started long before her and would keep going long after, even when names and faces changed.

When the timer rang, Grandma Verna pulled the pie from the oven. The crust was golden, and the juices bubbled up around the edges as she set it on the counter to cool, steam rising slowly and fogging the air between them. Verna watched the steam curl upward and wondered how many times she had stood in this exact spot, waiting for something to finish, waiting for answers that never quite came.

Sadie leaned in close and breathed deep. "It smells like heaven."

Grandma Verna smiled. "That's the orange talkin'."

She turned to fetch plates, but something made her stop as she passed the pantry. The door stood slightly ajar, just enough to catch her eye and tighten something in her chest. She stood there longer than necessary, listening to the quiet, feeling the shift in the room.

"Did you go in there earlier, baby?" she asked.

Sadie shook her head. "No, ma'am."

Grandma Verna hesitated before pushing the door open. The pantry was dim and lined with jars and tins, everything in its place except for one thing. A long, faded scarf hung from the top shelf, draped neatly over a jar of flour. The fabric was pale blue, frayed at the ends, and carried the faint scent of lilac that had no business being there. The smell reached her before the meaning did.

Grandma Verna's breath caught because she knew that scarf. Her hands trembled as she reached for it, her fingertips brushing the soft fabric like it might disappear if she touched it too hard. The years folded in on themselves in that moment, past and present pressing together until it was hard to tell where one ended, and the other began.

Sadie tilted her head. "Grandma? Whose is that?"

She swallowed before answering, her voice tight. "It belonged to somebody I loved very much."

"Your mama?" Sadie asked quietly.

Verna's eyes glistened as she nodded. "Yeah, baby. My mama."

She pressed the scarf to her chest and closed her eyes as the faintest hum filled the air, so soft it nearly blended into the warmth of apples and orange zest. The sound wrapped itself around the room, gentle and familiar, settling deep in Verna's bones where memory lived and waited. Sadie did not hear it, though she felt the room grow still, like the house itself was listening.

She heard it clearly and understood what it meant. She knew that voice anywhere. It was Thema's, and the song she hummed was more than a tune. It was a calling, patient and unyielding, reminding her that some things, once awakened, never truly go quiet.

Chapter Eight

The Awakening

That night, the smell of apple pie still lingered in the air, sweet and soft, clinging to the walls like memory itself. Rain had started again, tapping lightly against the windowpanes in a steady rhythm that felt almost alive. The sound followed Sadie as she brushed her teeth, as she changed into her nightgown, and as she crawled beneath the covers trying to make sense of the day.

Grandma Verna had gone to bed early, her scarf folded neatly at the end of her dresser, placed with care rather than fear. Sadie could hear her soft snore drifting down the hall, steady and familiar. The house, for once, felt peaceful, or at least it was pretending to be. Shadows rested where they belonged, and nothing seemed to move without reason.

Sadie lay in her bed with the doll pressed tightly against her chest, its body cool and still beneath her fingers. She stared at the ceiling, tracing faint cracks with her eyes as her thoughts wandered. The scarf kept returning to her mind, along with the hum that had followed it, and the look on her grandmother's face when she found it. Fear had been there, but so had something else... something quieter and deeper like recognition.

The clock ticked softly beside her bed. One second passed, then another, then another, each one stretching longer than the last. The rhythm began to change, blending into something else, something softer and older. A sound crept into the room so gently that Sadie wondered if she was imagining it.

A hum.

This one did not belong to Thema. This hum was lower and deeper, vibrating beneath the quiet as if it rose from the ground itself steadily and patiently... as if it had been waiting for her to notice. Sadie's eyelids grew heavy, and before she could fight the pull, sleep claimed her.

When she opened her eyes again, she was standing barefoot in a wide open field. The ground beneath her feet was damp and cool, grass bending under her toes as mist curled around her ankles. The air shimmered faintly, and the sky stretched wide and golden above her. There was no sun and no moon, only a glow that seemed to come from everywhere at once, wrapping the land in warmth. The wind brushed her face and carried with it the faint scent of lilac, cinnamon, and earth after rain. The smell felt familiar, comforting, like it belonged to her. In the distance, trees swayed slowly, their branches moving in unison as though bowing to something unseen.

Then Sadie saw her.

An old woman stood beneath a tree so ancient it seemed to touch the sky itself. Her presence filled the space around her, tall and radiant, rooted and alive. Silver hair was braided neatly down her back, and a shawl of many colors rested across her shoulders. Deep purples, rich golds, and soft blues shimmered within the fabric like starlight woven into cloth. Her eyes, though aged, glowed bright and steady, like candle flames that refused to flicker.

"Come here, child," the woman said, her voice gentle yet powerful, carrying the weight of thunder softened by silk.

Sadie hesitated, her heart pounding, though fear did not take hold. "Who are you?" she asked.

The woman smiled, slowly and knowingly. "You already know me. I have been with you since your first breath."

Sadie took a few careful steps closer. The woman's presence felt heavy but warm, like the air before rain, full of promise and warning all at once.

"Are you my grandma?" Sadie asked.

The woman chuckled softly, the sound rolling through the field like a breeze. "I am her mother's... mother's... mother. They called me Bibi."

Sadie's breath caught in her chest. "Bibi."

The name settled into her bones, sacred and familiar, as though it had always belonged to her. Bibi knelt before her, the shawl slipping from her shoulders and pooling onto the ground like light made solid. She took Sadie's hand and pressed something small into her palm. The object was smooth and cool at first, shaped like a circle and carved from bone. Etched into its surface was a symbol of a tree with its roots spiraling downward into water.

"This belongs to the one who listens," Bibi said softly. "You have been listening longer than you know."

Sadie curled her fingers around the pendant, feeling its weight. "Why are you here?" she asked.

Bibi's smile softened. "Because blood remembers even when the world forgets. Your grandmother carries the memory. Your mother runs from it. You were born to awaken what they could not finish."

Sadie shook her head slowly. "I don't understand what that means."

"You will," Bibi said, her voice steady and kind. "Each dream will show you more. Each song will open what was once closed."

Sadie looked around the glowing field. "Is my mama here too? Or the lady from the mirror?"

The wind shifted at that, sweeping through the grass and lifting the hem of Bibi's shawl.

"Thema wanders," Bibi said quietly. "Her story remains unfinished, her spirit restless. She stays near you, bound by song, by the doll, by love that did not die when her body did."

Bibi rose to her feet as the air around them began to tremble. The trees swayed harder now, their leaves whispering words Sadie could not understand. The pendant in Sadie's hand grew warm and pulsated softly against her skin.

Bibi's voice deepened, taking on the rhythm of prayer. "When the wind speaks your name, answer. When the ground hums beneath your feet, listen. You are the bridge, child, the living space between what was lost and what will be found."

The golden sky flickered, light rippling like water.

Bibi stepped forward and cupped Sadie's cheek. "Tell Verna I am proud. Tell her the line still stands."

A smile spread across her face, wide and beautiful, filled with knowing. "Tell your mother it is time to come home."

Sadie gasped and woke.

Her room was dark, rain still tapping softly against the window. Her heart raced as she realized her hand was clenched tightly against her chest. Slowly, she opened her fingers.

Her breath caught.

Resting in her palm was the pendant. It was small, bone white, and warm to the touch.

In the corner of the room, the doll sat watching, perfectly still, its diamond eyes reflecting the faintest flicker of gold that had no clear source.

The hum returned, low and steady, settling deep inside Sadie like a promise.

Chapter Nine
The Return

The next morning came heavy with gray clouds and a silence that seemed to settle into the bones of the house. The storm from the night before had passed, yet its memory lingered in the air, leaving behind a thick, damp smell of earth and lilacs that always appeared after something sacred had moved through the space. The light outside was muted, filtered through low clouds that refused to lift, casting the world in shades of silver and shadow.

Grandma Verna sat at the kitchen table with her scarf draped over her shoulders, the fabric wrapped close as if it offered protection. Her hands rested near a mug of coffee that had long since gone cold, though she had not taken a single sip. Her eyes stayed fixed on the window, watching rainwater drip slowly from the eaves, listening for sounds that could not be heard by most people. She felt the familiar weight press against her chest, the same feeling she had carried since childhood, the knowing that something was about to arrive whether she was ready or not.

Sadie sat beside her, unusually quiet, her small body still in a way that did not match her age. One hand rested in her lap while the other traced the outline of the pendant hidden beneath her nightgown. It felt warm against her skin, steady and alive, like it carried a pulse of its own. Her thoughts drifted between the dream she had woken from and the morning unfolding around her. She wanted to speak, to explain, to ask why her heart felt so full and so heavy at the same time. The house felt alert, listening in a way that made words feel fragile.

Neither of them spoke. Silence filled the space between them, thick and deliberate.

The stillness broke when the sound of tires crunching against gravel reached the yard. The noise felt sharp against the quiet, followed by the solid slam of a car door. Verna's fingers curled slightly against the table as recognition settled deep in her chest.

"She's here," she whispered, the words slipping out like a prayer and a warning all at once.

Sadie's head snapped up, her heart leaping painfully in her chest. She rushed to the window just as the front gate creaked open, its familiar groan echoing across the damp yard. A woman stepped out of the car, tall and brown skinned, her posture straight despite the weariness etched into her face. Her movements were careful, measured, as though she were bracing herself for what waited beyond the gate. Her hair was pulled back into a neat bun, her coat buttoned tightly to her chin, shielding her from more than the cold air.

"Mama," Sadie cried, her voice cracking as joy rushed up faster than she could contain it.

She ran for the door before Grandma Verna could speak. The porch boards were slick beneath her feet, and the grass soaked through her slippers as she crossed the yard. Her mother bent just in time to catch her, wrapping her arms tightly around Sadie and holding on as though letting go might undo the moment. The scent of perfume mixed with rain and long travel clung to her coat, unfamiliar yet deeply comforting.

"Hey, my baby," her mother said softly, her voice trembling despite her effort to sound strong. "Look at you. Taller already. Still got that same wild hair."

Sadie buried her face into her mother's shoulder, breathing her in like she might disappear again if she did not. "You came back," she whispered.

"I told you I would," her mother replied, pressing a kiss to her forehead. "Some things just take longer than we want."

From the porch, Verna watched quietly, her expression unreadable. Years of worry, regret, and prayer moved behind her eyes, though her face remained still.

"Come on inside," she said after a moment. "It's time we sit down."

Inside, the house felt different with all three of them present, smaller and fuller at the same time. The walls seemed closer, the air heavier, as though the house itself was paying attention. Verna poured coffee for her daughter, tea for herself, and placed a plate of leftover pie in front of Sadie. The scent was sweet and familiar, though Sadie barely touched it, nudging the crust with her fork as her thoughts drifted inward.

Sadie's mother sat stiffly at the table, her shoulders tight, her hands folded together as if holding herself in place. Her eyes traveled slowly around the room, taking in the details she had tried to forget.

"Mama told me what's been goin' on," she said finally, her gaze settling on Sadie. "About you seein' things. Hearin' things."

Sadie said nothing. Her fingers pressed lightly against the pendant beneath her shirt, feeling its warmth steady her breathing.

Her mother sighed. "Baby, I don't want you carryin' old stories that don't belong to you. This thing about being chosen is just a folk tale. Somethin' our people used to say to keep children close."

Grandma Verna's eyes darkened. "It ain't no tale, and you know that."

Her daughter turned sharply. "Mama, please. Not this again."

"It's always been this," Grandma Verna said calmly. "You can run from it, but you can't erase it."

Her daughter rubbed her temples, frustration breaking through her composure. "I left to keep her safe. Every generation, it takes somethin' from us."

Sadie's chest tightened. "Takes what?" she asked.

Grandma Verna answered softly. "Peace."

Sadie's mother reached across the table and squeezed her hand gently. "Baby, what you saw was just a dream."

Sadie shook her head. "It wasn't a dream. I saw her. I saw both of them."

Her mother froze. "Both?"

"Bibi and Thema," Sadie said quietly. "They talked to me. Bibi gave me this."

She pulled the pendant from beneath her nightgown, letting it rest in her palm as the light caught its surface.

Her mother's breath caught. One hand lifted instinctively toward her chest before dropping back to the table. "That can't be," she whispered. "That pendant's been gone for years."

"It was never gone," Grandma Verna said. "It was waitin'."

Her daughter turned toward her, eyes sharp with accusation and fear. "You knew."

"I prayed I was wrong," Grandma Verna replied. "Blood always finds its way home."

Tears filled Sadie's eyes before she could stop them. "Mama, I don't care about any of this. I just want you here."

Her mother brushed a tear from Sadie's cheek. "I'm here now."

The words sounded right, yet her voice trembled because she knew the truth even as she spoke. This was not a story meant to fade. This was a legacy waking up.

The afternoon light dimmed as the day dragged on. Rain began again, tapping steadily against the windows. Grandma Verna sat by the window with the pendant resting in her palm, its warmth steady. Across the room, Sadie's mother stood near the door, her coat half buttoned as though she were already preparing to leave.

"Please don't go," Grandma Verna said softly. "Not yet."

"I don't want her hearin' any more of this," her daughter replied. "She's too young."

"She understands more than you did. She listens."

Her daughter's voice sharpened. "I was born into this, and I chose to leave it."

"And what did it give you?" Grandma Verna asked. "Peace or emptiness?"

Her daughter looked away. "It gave me control."

"She ain't scared. She's curious."

Tears filled her daughter's eyes. "I saw what this did to you."

"You can't stop what's in her blood," Grandma Verna said. "The gift don't ask permission."

"This is a curse," her daughter said. "Don't you remember what it did to Thema?"

Grandma Verna met her gaze. "That's why I prayed for a child strong enough to finish what she started."

Her daughter shook her head. "She's my child."

"And she's theirs too," Grandma Verna said quietly.

Her daughter reached for the door. "If you love her, you'll let her forget."

"If I love her, I'll make sure she remembers."

The screen door creaked as Sadie's mother stepped into the rain, her figure fading down the road beneath the streetlights. Grandma Verna remained where she was, the pendant warm in her palm, her chest aching with the familiar weight of knowing too much and being able to stop nothing.

She whispered to the empty room, "She don't hear it."

The wind pressed gently against the windowpane, carrying a low hum in response.

Grandma Verna smiled through her tears. "But Sadie does."

Chapter Ten

The Tree That Calls

The night pressed softly against the windows, thick and unmoving, as if the darkness itself had settled in to listen. The moon hung low in the sky, pale gold against the deep blue, casting long shadows across the yard. Crickets whispered from the grass in uneven rhythms, and somewhere far off, thunder murmured low and slow. The sound carried no threat, only a reminder, like the earth clearing its throat.

Sadie slept restlessly beneath her quilt, her small body turning from side to side. Sleep no longer came gently to her. Her dreams arrived in waves now, heavy with color and sound, folding memory and imagination together until she could no longer tell where one ended and the other began. Some nights she saw her great-grandmother, Thema, standing beneath the oak tree, her scarf lifting in an unseen breeze. Other nights, she saw Bibi's shawl floating across a wide open field, glowing softly as it moved, as though stitched from light itself.

Tonight felt different.

Tonight, the dreams sharpened.

The air itself seemed to hum, low and steady, filling the spaces between her breaths.

Sadie stirred when the sound of her name reached her through sleep.

"Sadie..."

The voice was soft and tender, familiar in a way that made her chest ache. It came from outside her window, carried on the night air like a whisper meant only for her. Her eyes fluttered open, blinking against the pale moonlight filtering through the curtains. The room looked the same as always, yet everything felt altered, as though the walls were holding their breath.

The doll still sat on the dresser with its glassy eyes fixed in her direction. The pendant resting against her chest pulsed faintly beneath her nightgown, warm and rhythmic, like a heartbeat that did not belong to her alone.

The voice came again.

"Sadie... come."

Her breath caught as she pushed herself upright, pulling the blanket close to her chest. The air in the room shimmered faintly, bending the moonlight just enough to make her blink again. For a brief moment, movement reflected in the glass of the window.

Two shapes stood there.

One tall and elegant.

One wrapped in soft, glowing fabric.

Bibi and Thema.

Their voices overlapped, one deep and steady, the other gentle as wind moving through leaves.

"It's time."

Sadie slid from the bed, her feet finding her slippers by memory. She moved slowly and carefully, the way children do when they know the house is asleep and do not want to wake it. The wooden floor creaked beneath her steps, yet she did not stop. The pull was too strong to resist. It was not fear and not curiosity, but something sacred that settled deep in her chest and guided her forward.

She opened her bedroom door and stepped into the hallway, dimly lit by moonlight spilling through the small window at the top of the stairs. The air smelled faintly of rain and lilac, cool and familiar, like a memory she could not quite place. She paused when she reached Grandma Verna's door.

Her grandmother slept soundly inside, her breathing slow and even, her face peaceful in the soft glow of the moon. Sadie lifted her hand toward the doorknob, thinking to wake her, thinking she should not do this alone.

The whisper came again, closer now.

"Come, child of our blood."

Sadie's hand fell away from the door.

She descended the stairs one careful step at a time, the pendant glowing faintly against her chest as it warmed. The house felt alive around her. The air hummed softly, the walls seemed to breathe, and the curtains stirred even though the windows were closed. The familiar space felt older somehow, like it was remembering things she had only just begun to learn.

When she reached the back door, she stopped.

Through the glass, the oak tree stood tall and ancient, its thick trunk rising from the earth like a pillar. Its branches stretched wide toward the sky like open arms. At its base, a faint golden light pulsed slowly, brightening and dimming in time with the hum filling her ears.

Sadie opened the door and stepped outside.

The grass was damp beneath her feet, cool and slick with dew. The night wind brushed her skin, sweet and clean, carrying the scent of earth and orange peels from the kitchen scraps Grandma Verna had buried earlier that day. Moonlight washed over the yard, and the oak tree glowed faintly from within, a golden shimmer rippling up the bark like water finding its way to the surface.

With every step closer, the voices grew clearer.

"Do not fear us."

"You are the bridge."

"What was lost will find its way through you."

Sadie's eyes filled with tears. She did not understand every word, yet she understood the feeling behind them. Love surrounded her, vast and heavy, pressing into her chest until it almost hurt.

The air shimmered before her, bending and folding until two figures stepped forward from the light.

Thema appeared first, young and beautiful, her scarf floating behind her like mist. Her eyes held sorrow and wonder, pride and regret woven together. Beside her stood Bibi, her shawl heavy with light, her presence steady and grounding. They stood side by side, ancestors made whole through memory and faith.

"Sadie," Thema said softly, her voice trembling. "I tried to finish what began long ago. My voice was silenced too soon. You must carry what I could not."

Bibi's gaze never wavered. "I will guide you," she said. "As I once guided her."

Sadie's lip quivered as she shook her head. "I don't know what to do."

Bibi smiled gently. "You don't have to know. You only have to listen."

Thema reached out, her hand hovering just above Sadie's heart. The pendant flared brighter, its warmth spreading through her chest. "When the tree calls again," she whispered, "follow the roots. They will lead you to the truth."

Sadie blinked.

The light shifted, and both women began to fade, dissolving back into the glow pouring from the earth.

"Wait," Sadie cried. "Don't go."

Their voices overlapped one final time, soft and certain.

"We never left."

The light vanished.

Sadie stood alone beneath the oak, the night settling back into its quiet rhythms. Her cheeks were damp, her heart pounding hard enough to make her dizzy. She turned toward the house and froze.

Grandma Verna stood in the doorway, wrapped in her robe, the night air lifting the edge of her scarf. Her eyes were heavy with sadness, but there was no surprise in them.

"I told you," Grandma Verna said softly. "They always come when the wind changes."

Sadie ran to her and buried her face against her chest. "I saw them, Grandma. I saw both of them."

Grandma Verna stroked her hair gently, holding her close. "I know, baby. I felt it."

Her voice trembled as she added, "The tree only calls when it's almost time."

Sadie lifted her head. "Time for what?"

Grandma Verna looked toward the oak tree, her eyes glistening in the moonlight.

"For one of us to go home."

Chapter Eleven

A Different Kind Of Morning

The morning came soft and golden, the kind that tricked the heart into believing the world was still safe and unchanged. The storm had moved on during the night, leaving the sky washed clean and pale. Sunlight streamed through the curtains in long glowing bands, catching dust that floated lazily through the air like tiny spirits drifting without purpose. Everything looked gentle and ordinary, which made the quiet feel all the more misleading.

Sadie stirred slowly beneath her blanket, turning her face into the pillow before blinking her eyes open. The faint smell of earth and apples still lingered in her room, clinging to the walls and her nightgown. For a moment, she stayed very still, listening. She always woke to the sound of Grandma Verna humming in the kitchen, a low, comforting tune that wrapped itself around the house and let everyone know the day had begun.

That sound never came.

There was no shuffle of feet in the hallway. There was no clatter of dishes or hiss of coffee heating on the stove. The house held its breath in a way that felt unfamiliar.

Sadie sat up and rubbed her eyes, her small body stretching against the chill of the early air. Her heart fluttered with a strange mix of comfort and something she could not name yet. She waited another moment, listening harder, hoping the sounds would return if she gave them time.

"Grandma?" she called softly.

No answer followed.

She slipped her feet into her slippers and smoothed her nightgown, deciding to surprise Grandma Verna the way Grandma Verna sometimes surprised her. The thought made her smile, and she nodded to herself like the plan had already been approved.

"I'll make breakfast today," she whispered, pleased with the idea.

The floorboards creaked beneath her feet as she made her way down the stairs. The air felt cool and light, the way it does after a night filled with heavy dreaming. Sunlight spilled across the front door, landing on the family photos lining the wall. Sadie slowed as she passed them, studying each familiar face. Grandma Verna stood in one picture as a young woman, proud and steady. Her mother appeared in another, smiling wide and carefree. At the end hung an old black and white photograph of Thema standing near a tree, her expression calm and knowing.

Sadie reached out and touched the frame gently before continuing toward the kitchen.

The house smelled faintly of last night's pie, apples and cinnamon and sugar mixing with the scent of morning dew drifting in through the cracked window. On the counter, beneath a folded towel, sat what remained of the pie they had baked together. The crust had softened overnight, but the sweetness filled the air like a reminder.

Sadie smiled. "Grandma forgot to put it away."

She lifted the towel and carefully cut herself a small slice, just enough to taste. She placed it neatly on one of the floral plates Grandma

Verna loved. She poured herself a glass of milk the way Grandma Verna always did for her, then carried both to the kitchen table.

The seat across from hers sat empty.

She took a bite. The flavor was soft and familiar, the faint tang of orange tucked beneath the cinnamon.

"Mmm," she whispered with a quiet giggle. "Still perfect."

After finishing, she wiped her hands carefully and looked around the kitchen. The house felt so still it almost seemed to be listening. The quiet pressed gently against her ears.

"I should make breakfast for Grandma too," she said aloud, as if the walls needed to hear the plan.

She stood on her tiptoes to reach the coffee tin, smiling when the beans rattled inside like small pebbles. She measured a scoop into the pot and filled it with water, remembering how Grandma Verna used to hum while waiting for it to boil. She cracked two eggs into the skillet and pulled out slices of bread for toast. Her movements were clumsy but focused. She wanted everything to be just right.

When the coffee began to perk, its aroma filled the kitchen, wrapping around her like a hug she did not realize she needed. She set the table neatly with two plates, two forks, and two napkins folded into careful squares. She placed Grandma Verna's favorite mug beside the coffee pot, the one with the small chip on the rim that Grandma Verna always said gave it character.

"Okay," Sadie whispered, looking over her work proudly. "Now I'll get her."

She walked down the hallway toward Grandma Verna's room, the morning light trailing behind her like a soft ribbon. The air grew quieter with every step, the kind of quiet that made her slow down without knowing why. Her heart beat a little faster as she reached the door.

She knocked softly.

"Grandma?"

No sound answered.

Sadie pushed the door open just enough to peek inside. The curtains were half drawn, and the room glowed gently with the light of sunrise. Grandma Verna lay on her side, her scarf draped loosely over her shoulder, her face turned toward the window. Her hands were folded beneath her chin, peaceful and still.

"Grandma," Sadie said, stepping closer. "I made breakfast. You can sleep in, but I got coffee waitin' for you."

No answer came.

Sadie frowned and took another small step forward, the floor creaking beneath her slippers.

"Grandma?" she whispered again.

She reached the bedside and touched Grandma Verna's hand. It felt cool, not cold, but not warm either. Just still.

Sadie's heart began to pound. "Grandma, wake up," she said softly, shaking her hand. "I made your favorite pie. Coffee too. You gotta taste it."

The silence in the room deepened.

Sadie shook her hand again, harder this time. "Grandma, please."

Her voice cracked as fear finally found its way into her chest.

When she looked closer, she saw it. The faint smile on Grandma Verna's lips carried peace instead of pain. A single tear had dried at the corner of her eye.

Sadie pressed both hands over Grandma Verna's, whispering, "No, no, no."

The pendant around her neck grew warm. A breeze slipped through the half open window and brushed her cheek. It smelled like lilacs and apple pie.

Sadie turned toward the window, tears blurring her eyes. For the briefest moment, she saw Thema standing by the oak tree. Grandma Verna stood beside her, whole and radiant. Behind them, Bibi glowed faintly, her shawl open like wings.

They stood together in the golden light, faces calm and full of love.

Thema lifted her hand and whispered something Sadie could not hear, yet she understood it all the same.

Grandma Verna was not gone.

She had simply gone home.

Sadie knelt beside the bed and held Grandma Verna's hand against her cheek. "I love you, Grandma," she whispered through her tears. "I'm gonna finish what you started. I promise."

The wind stirred the curtains again, soft and tender. Somewhere outside, the oak tree rustled in response.

A faint hum filled the room, gentle and low, the sound of three voices moving together in perfect harmony. Beneath it, Sadie's own breath joined in, quiet and trembling, marking the beginning of a song she did not yet know she had been born to sing.

Chapter Twelve

The Awakening of Thema

The house was still in a way Sadie had never known before. The quiet felt heavy and full, pressing against the walls as though the space itself were waiting. Morning had risen fully now, sunlight spilling across the floorboards and climbing the bed where Grandma Verna lay. The light touched her face gently, smoothing the lines of age and worry until she looked almost younger, as if rest had finally claimed her.

Sadie had not moved from Grandma Verna's side since the moment she understood. Her small hand remained folded into her grandmother's, fingers laced tightly, as though she could hold her there by will alone. Her legs were stiff from kneeling so long, yet she did not notice the ache. Leaving felt impossible. Letting go felt worse.

Outside, the wind stirred the branches of the oak tree. Its whisper moved through the walls like breath passing from room to room. The sound carried memory with it, old and familiar. The hum that had filled the house through generations rose again, low and steady, vibrating through the wood and settling deep into Sadie's bones.

Sadie lifted her head slowly, her tear-streaked face catching the light.

"Grandma," she whispered.

The voice that answered was not Grandma Verna's.

It was softer and younger, trembling like wind moving through reeds.

"She's with me now."

Sadie turned, her heart thudding painfully in her chest. The air near the doorway shimmered, bending the light as though the room itself had exhaled a memory. The space shifted slowly and gently until it took shape.

A woman stood there.

She was barefoot and dressed in a white gown that fluttered though no air moved. Her hair was braided down her back, streaked with dust and moonlight. Her skin glowed faintly, not like fire, but like something remembered rather than seen.

Sadie rose to her knees, her voice shaking. "Thema?"

The woman blinked, and confusion widened her eyes. "How do you know my name?"

Sadie clutched the pendant at her neck, its warmth steadying her. "Because you told me. In my dreams. By the tree."

Thema's brow furrowed as she looked down at her hands. They trembled slightly. "Dreams," she murmured. "That's what this feels like. I keep waking, but I'm never awake."

Her gaze drifted to Grandma Verna's still form on the bed, and her breath caught.

"Mama," she whispered.

The word fell apart in her mouth. She stepped forward, each movement slow, her feet barely touching the floor. "I was too late," she said, her voice trembling like glass. "I thought if I found my way back, I could fix what was broken."

Sadie's throat tightened. "You did come back. She saw you. She knew."

Tears shimmered in Thema's eyes. They never fell, only glistened like dew clinging to leaves. "She forgave me before I ever asked. That kind of love binds and frees all at once."

Light shifted in the room. Dust swirled slowly in the air, catching the sunlight.

Thema turned toward Sadie, her expression filled with grief and wonder woven together. "You called me here," she said softly. "Your song reached me where even silence could not. When you sang, I heard my own name again after all these years."

Sadie swallowed hard. "I didn't mean to call you. I just wanted Grandma Verna to wake up."

Thema smiled gently. "Love does not always bring back who you want. Sometimes it brings who you need."

She knelt in front of Sadie, the faint shimmer of her body casting soft light across the bedspread. "You look just like her," she whispered. "Like Grandma Verna when she was small. Same eyes. Same stubborn heart."

Sadie's lip trembled. "You remember?"

"I remember pieces," Thema said quietly. "The laughter. The tree. The doll Bibi gave me. The night everything went dark."

Her voice wavered. "I do not remember why."

Sadie lowered her gaze, her fingers tracing the pendant's carved surface. "Bibi said when the tree calls again, the roots will tell the truth."

Recognition flickered across Thema's face. "The roots," she whispered. "That is where it began."

The wind outside rose suddenly, rattling the windows. The oak tree groaned as its branches scraped lightly against the house. Thema's form shimmered and flickered between the visible and the unseen.

"She's here," Thema whispered. "Bibi is calling."

Sadie reached for her hand. It felt cold, soft, and almost weightless. "Please do not go yet."

Thema smiled faintly. "I am not gone. I have only been lost. If I follow her, maybe I will remember."

Her hand began to fade, the light around her dimming.

Sadie held tighter. "What if I can help you remember?"

Thema looked at her with something between pride and sorrow. "Then you will have to be brave. What I forgot lives deep, buried where the world does not want it found."

Sadie nodded, tears spilling freely now. "I will find it."

Thema leaned forward and pressed her forehead gently to Sadie's. Her voice became a whisper against Sadie's ear.

"Then follow the roots, little one. They remember what we buried."

The light folded inward, collapsing like breath drawn back into the chest.

When Sadie opened her eyes again, the room was empty.

Only Grandma Verna remained, still and peaceful.

The window stood wide open now, the curtains lifting softly in the breeze. Outside, the oak tree swayed gently. The soil at its base looked dark and freshly stirred, as though something beneath had begun to wake.

Sadie rose slowly and moved to the window. The pendant at her chest glowed faintly, warm against her skin. The wind brushed her face and carried a whisper that sounded like three voices woven into one.

"It is not the end, Sadie. It is the beginning."

Sadie closed her eyes and whispered back, her voice steady despite the tears.

"I'm listening."

Chapter Thirteen

The Roots Remember

Night fell slow and heavy over the house. The moon rose behind a thin veil of clouds, pale and watchful, casting long silver shadows across the yard. The oak tree loomed larger than ever, ancient and alive, its branches whispering in a language older than words.

Sadie sat on the edge of her bed, still dressed in her nightgown. The window was open, and cool air brushed against her face, carrying the faint smell of damp soil and lilacs. Sleep would not come. Every time she closed her eyes, she saw them - Bibi, Grandma Verna, and Thema - their faces woven into the wind, their voices repeating the same message.

"Follow the roots."

She glanced toward the dresser. The doll sat there as always, its diamond eyes reflecting the moonlight, still and knowing. The pendant around her neck felt warm again, pulsing faintly, as if keeping time with the rhythm of the earth itself.

Sadie stood and let her bare feet touch the cold floor. The house creaked softly around her, yet fear did not follow. That part of her had already changed.

She moved quietly down the hall and paused outside Grandma Verna's room. Grandma Verna lay in her bed, peaceful and still, a small smile resting on her face in her final sleep. Sadie leaned closer and whispered, "I'll make you proud, Grandma," before closing the door with care.

Downstairs, the house seemed to sigh with every step she took. Old wood and old memories stirred in the corners, carrying the weight of spirits that had never truly left. Sadie slipped on her slippers and pulled Grandma Verna's shawl around her shoulders. Then, she stepped outside.

The night greeted her like an old friend. The air felt cool and wet. Grass shimmered beneath the moon, bending under her feet. The oak tree stood at the center of the yard, its silhouette stretching across the ground like the shadow of a giant. Sadie stopped several steps away when she noticed the soil at its base. The earth there was darker than the rest, freshly disturbed, and her pulse quickened.

The pendant grew warmer against her skin. A hum rose from the ground, low and steady, no longer carried by the wind. The sound held the weight of something buried beneath layers of dirt and time, a song she somehow already knew.

Sadie knelt in the grass. The earth felt soft beneath her hands as she dug gently at first, then deeper, her small fingers pressing into damp soil. The smell of dirt and roots filled her nose, raw and ancient, almost sweet. Time slipped away as she worked, and the world grew quiet around her. Even the crickets seemed to hold their breath.

Her fingers brushed against something hard, and she froze. Her heart pounded in her ears as she carefully brushed soil aside until a shape emerged, round and smooth, wrapped in faded cloth. Sadie swallowed and pulled it free.

A wooden box rested in her hands, no bigger than Grandma Verna's Bible. The carvings along its edges were worn, yet the patterns remained visible. Spirals, trees, and a single symbol she recognized from her pendant traced the surface. Sadie ran her fingers over it and whispered, "You were waiting for me."

The wind stirred, and the oak's branches shivered. A whisper moved through the leaves, not in one voice but many.

"Open it, child."

Sadie hesitated, her hands trembling. The clasp was rusted shut, and the wood felt slick with moisture. She pressed her thumbs against it and pulled until it gave with a soft snap. Inside, wrapped in linen so old it nearly disintegrated, lay a bundle of letters tied with red thread. Beneath them rested a small, cold object, a tarnished locket worn smooth by time.

She lifted the letters first. The paper was fragile, its edges browned, yet the writing remained clear. Sadie unfolded one carefully and read the faded ink.

To Bibi,

The night they came for me, I buried this beneath the tree so our voices would never die. If I do not return, tell them, tell her, to listen when the wind speaks.

Thema

Tears filled Sadie's eyes. Her chest tightened as she pressed the letter to her heart.

The wind rose and carried with it the faint scent of lilacs and smoke. The pendant around her neck glowed brighter, flooding the yard with soft light. Within that glow, Thema appeared again, no longer flickering or lost. She stood fully before Sadie, her eyes shining, her face both sorrowful and radiant.

"You found it," Thema whispered. "The truth we buried."

Sadie looked up through tears. "You wrote the letters."

Thema nodded slowly. "I was silenced before I could tell them. The truth stayed in the ground, waiting for your hands."

Sadie held out the locket. "What's inside?"

Thema's expression softened. "Everything we lost."

Sadie opened it carefully. Inside rested a tiny lock of hair, golden brown and tightly curled, untouched by time. Etched into the metal behind it were words that should not have survived the years, yet spoke clearly to her heart.

The blood remembers.

Thema sank to her knees, her voice breaking. "Now I can rest. The work is not finished. The roots do not only remember. They grow, and you must protect what they hold."

Sadie nodded through her tears. "I will."

Thema smiled, her form glowing brighter. "Tell my mother I am free."

Light lifted with the wind, and Thema dissolved into countless motes that spiraled upward into the branches and disappeared into the stars.

Sadie remained kneeling by the tree long after the light faded. The wooden box rested in her lap, her hands shaking, her heart full. The earth beneath her felt quiet now, peaceful yet alive. Roots whispered beneath the soil, humming softly, carrying the voices of her ancestors through the ground and into her bones.

"I remember too," Sadie whispered.

The wind moving through the oak no longer sounded sad.

It sounded like home.

Sadie sat cross-legged near the roots, the wooden box resting in her lap. Her fingers trembled as she unfolded the next letter from the bundle. The paper felt fragile, soft as dried petals, its edges worn thin by time. The handwriting looped carefully across the page, graceful and deliberate, like someone writing through tears.

If this letter finds you, it means I did not make it home. I have not gone far. The ground knows my story, and the wind carries my name. The one who finds this will be the one who listens without fear. The line will continue through her.

Sadie traced the words with her fingertip, her chest tightening. "I'm the one," she whispered. "I listened."

She turned the page, noticing smudged lines where rain or tears had washed across the paper years ago. She leaned closer, holding the letter to the moonlight, and felt it then, the unmistakable sense of being watched.

Her breath hitched as she looked toward the fence at the edge of the yard.

Light flickered from the window of the house next door, belonging to Mr. Langston. He was an older man with kind eyes and a voice like gravel softened by time. He had lived there since before Sadie was born and was always nearby, trimming hedges, watering his garden, or waving when Grandma Verna hung laundry to dry. Sometimes he brought over a small bag of apples that had rolled from Grandma Verna's tree into his yard.

Now he stood still behind the glass, his hand resting against the window, his face half-lit by the lamp behind him. When he noticed Sadie looking back, he did not turn away. He nodded once, slow and deliberate, like a gesture of respect.

Sadie's heart thumped. She remembered seeing him at the funeral, standing quietly at the back of the church with his hat in hand. She had watched him wipe a tear from his cheek before slipping out the side door.

Seeing him now stirred something unexplainable in her chest, a familiarity she could not name. The pendant against her skin pulsed once, faintly, as if it recognized something too.

The light inside Mr. Langston's house went out, leaving only moonlight reflected on the glass. Sadie exhaled slowly and whispered, "Maybe he just misses Grandma too."

She turned back to the letters as the night wrapped around her again, the hush of wind through branches and the soft hum of the earth beneath her. She read until her eyelids grew heavy, the words of her ancestor settling into her like lullabies made of truth.

When she gathered the letters and placed them back into the wooden box, the pendant on her chest flickered once more with a warm glow, like the steady pulse of a heartbeat. Sadie sensed that Grandma Verna was not the only one watching over her now.

Across the fence, Mr. Langston stood at his window once more, staring into the night. His eyes, dark and remembering, caught the faint shimmer from Sadie's pendant through the trees.

He whispered to no one, "Bibi's line still breathes."

The wind carried his words through the branches of the oak, where something unseen listened and remembered.

Chapter Fourteen
The Blood Remembers

The morning came gray and quiet. A thin mist rolled over the yard, turning the oak into a shadowed figure beneath a silver sky. The air smelled faintly of wet bark and apples fallen into the grass.

Sadie sat at the kitchen table with the wooden box open in front of her. The bundle of letters lay across a linen cloth, the ink faded to brown, the paper soft and thin. Her fingers trembled each time she touched one, like she was holding a heartbeat instead of paper. The coffee pot still sat cold on the stove from the day before. She did not bother to heat it. Her world had slowed. Time itself felt fragile, the house filled with the presence of those who were gone but not gone at all.

The first letter she read was dated 1938. The handwriting was neat, the loops wide and steady.

Thema's.

> *Bibi,*
> *I think I am being followed. He comes to the gatherings and stands in the back where the candles burn low. He never speaks, but I feel his eyes. Jonas*

says not to worry, that he is just curious, but I know the difference between curiosity and hunger.

If anything happens, tell Mama not to wait by the tree.

I will come back when the wind calls my name.

Sadie swallowed hard. The paper smelled faintly of smoke and something older, like iron. She unfolded the next letter with shaking hands.

Tonight, the song will be sung. I feel it in my bones, the choosing. If I am the one, I will wear the scarf. Tell them not to fear. I have seen the sign in my dreams and the doll's eyes turning to light.

I am ready.

Her vision blurred as tears spilled over her lashes. This was the night Thema was taken. It was the night Grandma Verna had only heard whispers about but never fully spoken of.

The next letter was smaller, written in haste. The ink had bled where rain must have hit the page.

Bibi, they lied to me. It was not a ritual. It was a trap. The man who came for me was not a stranger. He wore Jonas's coat, but his face was not his.

The light went out before I could see the truth.

If I do not return, tell them to follow the roots.

The blood remembers.

Sadie's heart pounded so hard she thought it might burst. She pressed the letter to her chest and whispered the words aloud. *"The blood remembers."* She could feel it now – the connection, the ache, the echo of her great-grandmother's last breath settling into the soil beneath the oak.

The last letter in the bundle was written in another hand. The writing was strong and masculine, unfamiliar. The letter was unsigned.

Forgive me.

I did what I was told, not what I wanted. She was not meant to die. I only meant to frighten her, to stop the ritual before it spread. The others wanted the doll. They said it held power. I only wanted her to live. If the wind carries this to you, know that I never forgot her eyes. I see them in every dream. In every storm. I see them in the face of my son.

Sadie froze. Her breath caught in her throat.

I see them in the face of my son.

The words hung in the air like thunder. She read them again, slower this time, each word pressing deeper. Whoever wrote the letter, whoever took Thema, had a child.

A son.

Sadie turned toward the window. Across the fence, Mr. Langston's house stood still, the curtains drawn. A faint golden light flickered in the kitchen window, the same glow that had burned there the night before. Her pulse quickened. The neighbor, kind and quiet Mr. Langston, who had cried at the funeral and always gathered fallen apples, had eyes that looked almost like hers.

Brown, with rings of gold around the pupils. Just like the eyes in the locket.

The wind moved through the trees then, strong enough to rattle the panes. The pendant around Sadie's neck grew warm, glowing faintly beneath her shirt. She lifted it and stared at the engraved words inside.

The blood remembers.

For the first time, she understood. The past was not something behind her. It was here, living and breathing, watching. Her grandmother's prayers, Bibi's chant, Thema's voice, all of it lived inside her veins. The truth, the final truth, stood closer than she had ever imagined.

Sadie looked out the window one last time. Mr. Langston stood in his yard, gazing toward the oak. He lifted his hat slowly and respectfully, then turned and disappeared into the shadows.

Sadie whispered to the empty kitchen, "It's you, isn't it?"

Only the wind answered, carrying the hum of generations through the open window and into her bones.

Chapter Fifteen

The Mirror of Faces

The morning air felt heavier than usual, carrying the scent of damp leaves and wood smoke. The house was quiet, yet the quiet did not feel empty. It felt watchful.

The letters still lay open on the kitchen table, the ink faded but alive, their words echoing in Sadie's mind like a steady drumbeat. The blood remembers. The blood remembers.

Sadie stood by the window, her eyes fixed on the fence line where Mr. Langston's house sat in its usual stillness. The curtains were open now, and the golden light she had seen before had been replaced by the gray hush of dawn. She could see him through the glass, sitting at his kitchen table with his hands folded and his head bowed. The same stillness she had seen in Grandma Verna now rested in his posture.

Something in Sadie's chest pulled with quiet insistence. A knowing settled over her, steady and unavoidable. A thread tightened between two lives that were never meant to meet, yet always would.

She tucked the letters into the wooden box, slipped the pendant beneath her shirt, and stepped outside.

The grass was wet with dew, and the morning chill bit at her ankles as she walked barefoot across the yard. The oak tree stood behind her, silent and watchful, its branches stretching like an old guardian. Mr. Langston was already standing on his porch when she reached the fence. He looked like he had been waiting.

"Morning, Sadie," he said softly, his voice low and steady.

"Morning," she answered, her voice barely more than a whisper.

His gaze dropped to the box in her hands. "You been diggin' again."

Sadie hesitated, unsure whether to lie or tell the truth. His tone told her the truth was already known.

"Yes," she said. "I found letters. From Thema."

At the sound of the name, Mr. Langston's face went still. His eyes, dark brown with a ring of gold, flickered with something that looked like memory. He drew a slow breath. "I thought maybe that name would find its way back one day."

Sadie tilted her head. "You knew her?"

He looked away for a long moment before answering. "Not me. My father did."

Sadie's stomach tightened. "Your father?"

Mr. Langston nodded, his eyes fixed on the distance as though the truth was too heavy to face directly. "He was a young man then. Worked for the church down the hill. They told him he was helpin' stop somethin' evil. A ritual, they said. He did not know it was a lie until it was too late."

Sadie gripped the fence rail. "He was there when she died."

Mr. Langston closed his eyes, the lines around them deepening. "He was more than there, child. He carried the guilt his whole life. Said her eyes followed him in every storm. Before he passed, he told me, 'If you ever meet the child with her eyes, tell her I'm sorry.'"

Sadie's throat ached. Tears threatened, heavy and sharp. She stepped closer to the fence. "You cried at my grandma's funeral," she said quietly. "Why?"

He looked up at her then, his gaze heavy and tender. "Because I saw it happen again. A good woman goin' home before her time. I saw you standin' there, and I knew the blood don't forget."

Sadie stared at him as the wind lifted the hem of her nightgown. "You look like her," she whispered. "Thema - you have her eyes."

A faint, sad smile crossed his face. "Maybe that's why I couldn't look away when you moved in. Felt like seein' a ghost I'd been waitin' on."

He took a slow step forward, his voice softer now. "Your family carries power, child. Power never comes easy. Sometimes it's born through pain, through blood and truth finally speakin'."

Sadie nodded as tears slipped down her cheeks. "She forgave him," she said. "I know she did. I saw her. She said she could rest."

Mr. Langston's eyes glistened. He pressed a hand to his chest. "Then maybe I can rest too."

They stood there for a long while, separated by the old fence, two branches of the same root, bound by a history neither of them chose but both carried.

The wind rose, moving through the trees with a low, familiar hum. Sadie lifted her face toward it, her tears drying on her skin. The pendant beneath her nightgown glowed faintly, and Mr. Langston noticed it for the first time.

He stared, his breath catching. "That symbol."

Sadie lifted the pendant into view. "It's the same one on the letters."

He nodded slowly. "My father had it too. Burned into a wooden cross he kept until the day he died. He said it was the mark of forgiveness for those who carried the weight of what they broke."

The hum deepened, curling through the air like breath and song intertwined. Sadie smiled through her tears. "It's not just forgiveness," she said. "It's remembrance."

Mr. Langston studied her then, really looked, and saw not just a child but every woman who had come before her. He saw Bibi's strength, Grandma Verna's grace, and Thema's eyes.

The hum faded, replaced by the stillness of dawn. Mr. Langston's voice was rough when he spoke again. "If the roots remember, maybe the branches can heal."

Sadie nodded, her fingers tightening around the pendant. "That's what Grandma said too."

He gave her one last look, the kind that felt like a prayer, before stepping back from the fence. "Take care of yourself, Sadie," he said. "Take care of that tree. It holds more than memory now. It holds you."

She watched him disappear into his house, the door closing gently behind him. Sadie turned back toward the oak. The sun had risen higher, spilling gold across the roots and branches. The light touched her face, warm and steady, and for the first time since Grandma Verna's passing, peace settled into her chest.

The voices had gone quiet, not because they were gone, but because she finally understood.

The blood remembered.

Now, so did she.

Chapter Sixteen
The Doll's Breath

Mr. Langston's words followed Sadie into the night as heavy as prayer. The night after speaking with him, she could not sleep. The wind pressed softly against the windows, and the oak tree moaned outside like it was restless, too. The sound did not feel like the weather. The sound felt like something trying to speak without a mouth.

Sadie sat on the edge of her bed with her feet planted on the cold floor and her nightgown bunched at her knees. The wooden box rested beside her, closed now, yet she could still feel the weight of it as if it were open and watching. The letters inside had changed everything. The truth in those pages had shifted the air in the house. It had shifted the way her own name sounded in her head. The doll was perched on her dresser the way it always had, porcelain face smooth and calm, diamond eyes catching the moonlight through the blinds. The eyes were like tiny mirrors, sharp enough to hold secrets. Everything in the room looked the same, but nothing in the room felt the same. The air carried a thickness that made her breathe shallowly without meaning to. The quiet did not settle like peace. The quiet leaned in, watchful and patient, and waited for Sadie to do something.

Sadie reached beneath her nightgown and touched the pendant. The metal felt cool tonight for the first time in days. There was no warmth pulsing from it or a glow to light her skin. The silence of it should have comforted her, yet the stillness made her uneasy. The pendant had become her warning bell, the thing that told her when the unseen world drew near. It's quiet felt like the pause right before a storm breaks.

Her eyes lifted back to the dresser. The doll looked closer than before. Sadie blinked and studied the distance between the doll and the edge of the dresser. The doll had been placed near the back earlier. She tucked it safely away from where it might fall. The doll sat near the front now, close enough that one careless bump could send it tumbling.

Sadie frowned and whispered, "Did I move you?"

No answer came, yet a soft rustle shifted through the corner of the room. Her gaze snapped to the curtains. The fabric moved slightly, as if a hand had brushed it aside. Sadie sat very still, listening. The window was closed. She knew it was closed. She had checked it earlier, pressing her palms to the glass, locking it, sliding the latch until it clicked. The curtain shifted again anyway, slow and deliberate, the way a person moves when they do not want to be seen.

Sadie's throat tightened. Her voice came out smaller than she intended. "Who's there?"

The room stayed silent, yet the air changed, as if the question had been heard. The temperature dropped in a way that did not belong to the night air. Cold slid across her skin like water. A faint hum began, so low she almost thought it was in her head. The sound was not carried by the wind outside. The sound was inside the room, small and steady, vibrating like breath.

Sadie stood slowly, her knees weak, and her heartbeat loud in her ears. Her slippers scraped the floor as she took one step toward the dresser, then another. The hum grew stronger as she moved closer. The vibration felt gentle, yet it held a steadiness that made her stomach twist.

The sound reminded her of Grandma Verna's humming in the kitchen. It was the same slow rhythm that used to fill the house with safety, only this time it carried something deeper... something older.

Sadie stopped near the dresser and swallowed hard. "Grandma Verna," she whispered. "Is that you?"

The hum kept going.

The lamp on her nightstand flickered once. It flickered again, brighter than before, as if the bulb fought to stay alive. A third flicker came, then the hum cut off sharply, like someone had pressed a finger to its lips. The silence that followed felt thick enough to touch. Sadie's breath caught as she took a step back.

The doll's diamond eyes glowed faintly blue. The glow was not bright enough to light the room. The glow was bright enough to make the doll look awake. The blue pulse matched the beat of Sadie's heart. The light pulsed once, then dimmed. Sadie blinked hard, hoping she had imagined it. The doll's eyes stared back, clear and still now, as if nothing had happened.

Sadie's hands shook. "No," she whispered. "No, I ain't doin' this."

Her eyes shifted to the mirror across from her bed. The mirror looked darker than it should have, like night had thickened inside the glass. Sadie turned fully toward it, unable to stop herself. A cold rush slid through her body as she watched her own reflection stand there in the moonlight. Her reflection did not match her.

Sadie stayed still, yet the reflection tilted its head a moment too late. Sadie's lips parted, yet the reflection smiled a second after she did, slow and wrong, like it was learning her face. Sadie stumbled back and knocked into the dresser. The wooden box shifted and thumped softly against the wood. The doll toppled to the floor with a dull sound that felt too loud in the silence. The lamp went out completely, and the darkness swallowed everything.

Sadie stood frozen with her eyes wide and her breath shallow. Her heartbeat filled the room like thunder, loud enough to drown out thought. The moonlight should have slipped through the blinds, and shadows should have softened the corners, but the darkness held tight like a hand.

A whisper came from the floor, soft and broken, almost childlike. "Don't leave me."

Sadie dropped to her knees without thinking. Her hands searched through the darkness until her fingers brushed porcelain. Cold shot into her fingertips. The doll felt too cold. It was colder than the floor and colder than night air should be. The chill sank into her palm like it wanted to crawl under her skin.

Sadie pressed the doll to her chest. "I'm here," she whispered, voice shaking. "I'm right here."

The smell of earth rose suddenly, raw and damp, as if the ground beneath the oak had opened and breathed into the room. Sadie gagged softly, then held her breath, afraid that breathing too deeply would pull something into her lungs. Her fingers tightened around the doll's face, and she felt something gritty against the porcelain. Sadie brought the doll closer, squinting in the dark until her eyes adjusted. A streak of dirt stained the doll's cheek. The soil was dark and wet, the same soil from the base of the oak. It looked fresh, as if it had been smeared there moments ago.

Sadie shook her head. "How did you get that on you?" she whispered.

A soft creak sounded behind her, a slow groan of wood like someone shifting their weight in the room. Sadie turned her head in one sharp motion.

Nothing stood there.

No one stood there.

The air stayed full anyway.

Sadie crawled backward until her knees bumped the bed. She pulled herself up, still clutching the doll, and sat with her back against the headboard. The mirror stood across from her, calm again, matching her now. The smile was gone. The delay was gone. The glass looked normal.

Sadie did not believe it.

Sadie sat there breathing through her nose, trying to slow her heart down before it beat itself out of her chest. The doll felt heavier in her arms than it should have, like the porcelain had swallowed something. Her hands stayed locked around it, tight enough to make her fingers ache. She did not want to look away. She did not want to look too closely either.

The darkness in the room began to loosen, little by little. Moonlight slipped through the blinds again, thin and weak, laying pale lines across the bedspread. Shadows returned to their corners, settling as they belonged there. The silence stayed different, though, less empty and more aware. The house sounded like it was holding itself together, every beam and nail remembering it was old.

Sadie's eyes drifted back to the mirror. Her reflection stared straight ahead, still as a picture. Fear crept up her throat again. Her reflection blinked when she blinked this time, no delay, no wrong smile. The calmness of it made her uneasy, like the mirror was pretending.

Sadie swallowed. "I'm not scared of you," she whispered, even though her voice shook on the last word. "You hear me. I'm not."

The air near the dresser shifted, soft as a breath against the back of her neck. Sadie stiffened. Her grip tightened around the doll until the porcelain pressed cold into her skin.

A sound came, so faint she almost missed it. The sound was not a hum. The sound was more like a tiny scratch, like fingernails against wood, like something trying to climb out of a place it had been trapped too long. Sadie's eyes slid toward the floor where the doll had fallen.

A thin line of dirt stretched across the floorboards... it was not there before.

The line looked like something had been deliberately dragged from the dresser to the foot of her bed. The dirt was dark and wet, and the smell of it rose again, heavy and alive, like rain-soaked earth split open by roots.

Sadie whispered, "Stop."

The line did not move, yet the air pulsed as if it had listened. A second sound came, closer this time, softer than a footstep. The mattress dipped beside Sadie, just slightly, like someone had sat down on the edge of the bed. Sadie froze, every muscle locking. Her eyes stayed forward, fixed on the mirror, too afraid to turn her head.

Her breath came out in a shaky whisper. "Grandma Verna?"

No answer came. The air grew colder anyway, cool enough to raise bumps across her arms. The smell of lilac slid through the room, sweet and sharp at the same time, mixing with the damp earth smell until Sadie felt like she was sitting under the oak tree instead of in her bedroom.

Sadie's eyes filled with tears. "I don't know what you want from me," she whispered. "I'm tryin' to listen. I'm tryin' to do it right."

The pendant stayed quiet against her chest. The doll stayed still in her arms. The mattress lifted and the pressure was gone as quickly as it came. The room loosened again, yet Sadie knew the message had been delivered. Something had sat with her, something had listened, and something had decided she could hear it. Sadie wiped her cheeks with the back of her hand, smearing a little dirt across her skin without noticing. Her voice came out small, the way it did when she was a little girl asking for a nightlight.

"Please let me sleep."

The air softened. The mirror stayed calm. The line of dirt remained on the floor like proof. Sadie did not remember falling asleep again. Exhaustion pulled her down in the quiet hours, heavy and deep, the way grief does when it finally wins.

Morning arrived gray and heavy, the sky outside thick with clouds. Sadie woke with a start, heart racing, hands gripping the blanket as if she had been falling. The room looked normal again. The air smelled faintly of damp leaves and something sweet like apples left too long on the ground.

Sadie sat up quickly and looked down.

The doll was sitting upright on her pillow, hands folded neatly in its lap, eyes clear and bright as glass. No dirt marked its porcelain cheek. No streak stained its face. The doll looked clean, innocent, perfect.

Sadie's mouth went dry. "I did not put you there," she whispered.

Her hands felt stiff. She lifted them and stared.

Dried dirt streaked her palms, packed into the lines of her skin. The soil looked dark and rich, the same earth from beneath the oak. She rubbed her fingertips together, and flakes crumbled onto the blanket. Sadie's gaze dropped to her nails. Something pale clung beneath them. Sadie leaned closer, squinting. Thin, stringy bits curled under the tips of her nails, damp and alive.

Tiny roots.

Her stomach turned. She slid off the bed and rushed to the mirror, staring at her reflection in the morning light. Her face looked the same, yet her eyes looked older. Her cheeks were pale. Her lips trembled.

Sadie whispered, "What did I do?"

The pendant beneath her nightgown pressed against her chest, still cool, still quiet, as if it had nothing to say about what had happened. The doll sat behind her on the pillow, still and watching. Sadie backed away slowly, dirt still under her nails, roots still clinging to her skin, and understanding settled over her with a certainty that made her chest ache.

The night had not been a dream.

The roots had called her.

Something had followed her back.

Chapter Seventeen

The Chosen and the Curse

The day began like any other, yet the air inside the house felt wrong from the moment Sadie woke up. Sunlight filtered through the kitchen curtains, pale and thin, touching the edges of the table without warming it. The light looked tired, as though it had traveled too far to arrive fully. Outside, the oak stood still, its branches unmoving despite the faint breeze that stirred the grass. Sadie sat at the kitchen table with her hands folded in her lap. The doll rested in the chair across from her, propped carefully as if it had been seated there on purpose. Its porcelain face reflected the morning light, its diamond eyes fixed forward and unblinking.

Her mother moved quietly around the kitchen. Coffee brewed on the stove. A dish clinked softly in the sink. Every sound felt deliberate, as if silence were something to be avoided. It had been weeks since Grandma Verna's funeral. The house still felt like it was waiting for her to come back.

"Sadie," her mother said at last, glancing over her shoulder. Her voice sounded worn thin. "You been quiet all morning. You feel okay?"

Sadie shrugged without looking up. "Just tired."

Her mother followed her gaze to the doll and frowned. "You still sleepin' with that thing?"

Sadie traced a small circle on the tabletop with her finger. "It helps me dream."

Her mother exhaled slowly, resting her hands on the counter. "Dreams ain't always meant to be followed, baby. Some doors, once opened, don't close again."

Sadie lifted her head. Her eyes looked darker than usual, the gold around her pupils faint but present. "That's what Grandma said too," she replied quietly. "But she also said some doors don't open unless you knock."

The room went still.

Her mother turned slowly, her face tightening. "What did you say?"

Sadie blinked, suddenly uncertain. "I said Grandma told me that."

Before her mother could respond, the pendant beneath Sadie's shirt pulsed once, sharp and sudden.

The kitchen disappeared.

Sadie stood barefoot in a wide field beneath a bright sky. Tall grass brushed her knees as laughter rang through the air. Her mother's laughter. Younger. Freer. Sadie turned toward the sound, her heart lifting, but the laughter broke. A man's harsh and angry voice cut through the field. Her mother screamed. The grass flattened beneath running feet. A shadow fell across the ground. Sadie gasped as the vision shattered. She stumbled backward, knocking into the table. A mug crashed to the floor, shattering. Coffee spread across the tile like spilled ink.

Her mother rushed toward her. "Sadie? Sadie, what just happened?"

Sadie's chest heaved. Her hands trembled. "He hurt you," she whispered.

Her mother froze. "What did you say?"

"You were little," Sadie continued, her voice shaking. "You were hiding. Under the table. Grandma was yelling. He was yelling."

Her mother's face drained of color. "Stop," she said softly. "Stop right now."

But the images kept coming.

Sadie saw her mother curled into herself, crying into her hands. She saw Grandma Verna pulling her close, whispering prayers through clenched teeth. She felt fear that wasn't her own, pain that didn't belong to her body.

Her mother grabbed her shoulders. "Sadie, look at me."

Sadie screamed.

The pendant flared, heat searing against her skin. The lights flickered violently. The air filled with the smell of lilacs and smoke. The doll's eyes flashed blue, reflecting the glow like polished glass. Then... everything went silent. Sadie collapsed against her mother, sobbing.

Her mother held her tightly, shaking. "You don't know that," she whispered. "You couldn't."

Sadie looked up at her through tears. "I didn't want to," she said. "It just came."

Her mother pressed her palms to her temples. "You have to stop listening. You have to let them rest."

Sadie shook her head. "They won't stop talking.

That night, Sadie sat on the floor of her bedroom, the doll resting in her lap.

Rain tapped softly against the window. The house creaked and settled around her. Shadows gathered in the corners of the room, stretching and shifting as the lamp flickered.

"Make it stop," Sadie whispered. "Please."

The doll stared back at her. For a moment, nothing happened. Then the doll's lips curved, just slightly. The air grew cold. Sadie turned toward the mirror. Her reflection lagged behind her movements, delayed by a breath too long. She leaned closer, her heart pounding. The reflection changed. The face staring back was not hers. It was Thema.

"You're losing control," Thema said softly. "The power doesn't belong to you alone. It remembers everyone who carried it."

Sadie's hands shook. "Then tell me how to stop."

Thema's eyes darkened. "You can't stop it."

The reflection leaned closer, her voice steady and certain. "You can only choose what you become."

The pendant pulsed.

A crack split the mirror from top to bottom.

The doll, still resting in Sadie's lap, began to hum.

Chapter Eighteen

The Bloodline's Debt

The rain returned that night, heavy and relentless, drumming against the roof in a rhythm that felt too deliberate to be weather alone. Thunder rolled close enough to rattle the windows, and lightning tore through the sky in sharp flashes that lit Sadie's room in white and silver before plunging it back into darkness. Shadows leapt along the walls and ceiling, stretching and recoiling as though the house itself were breathing.

Sadie sat in the center of her bed, her posture stiff, her knees drawn close. The doll rested upright against her legs, its porcelain face tilted toward her, unblinking. The pendant at her chest pulsed faintly beneath her nightgown, warming and cooling in time with the storm outside. She had not eaten since morning. She had barely spoken all day. Listening had taken the place of everything else, because now the voices were no longer whispers slipping in at the edges of her thoughts. They were layered, overlapping, constant, pressing against her mind with the weight of generations.

Sadie.

Remember us.

Pay what was owed.

She pressed her hands over her ears, her breath shallow and uneven, and whispered for them to stop. The plea went unanswered. The mirror across the room shimmered, her reflection blurring and sharpening in uneven pulses. Sometimes she saw her own face, pale and frightened. Sometimes she saw Thema's eyes staring back at her, filled with sorrow. Other times, the reflection shifted into something unfamiliar, its features refusing to settle, as though no single face could hold it.

The temperature in the room dropped, cold sliding along her arms and settling deep in her chest. The doll's diamond eyes flared blue, brighter than they had ever been, and the hum that once felt like comfort sharpened into something tense and restless. It vibrated through her ribs like it wanted escape.

"Grandma?" Sadie whispered, her voice barely sound. "Bibi?"

No one answered.

Only the hum remained, and beneath it, the slow, steady sound of breathing that did not belong to her. The lamp beside the bed flickered, dimmed, then steadied, and the hum shaped itself into words that scraped against her thoughts. The voice was not loud, but it was absolute.

"You opened the ground, child. You woke us all."

Sadie slid backward until her shoulders met the wall, her hands trembling at her sides. She shook her head, tears blurring her vision. She told them she only wanted the truth, that she only wanted to help. The answer came without mercy.

"Truth carries a price. Someone must always pay it."

Heat surged from the pendant, spreading through her chest like fire, and the doll's head tilted just enough for Sadie to notice. Its lips parted, and her name slipped out in Thema's voice. Panic clawed up her throat as Sadie told herself it was lying, that it was not her, that it could not be. The doll smiled anyway, faint and empty, and its voice deepened, folding over itself until it sounded like many speaking as one. Thema had opened the door. Sadie had walked through it. This was what remained.

Light burst from the pendant, slamming Sadie into the wall and knocking the air from her lungs. The mirror shattered, glass scattering across the floor in a ringing spray. From the broken reflection, smoke gathered and twisted, pulling itself into the outline of a woman whose face refused to form, her features shifting as though erased again and again. The voice that came from her filled the room. She said she was the first, before Bibi, before Thema, before the line learned how to bury what frightened it. She said they saved themselves by passing her power down and forgetting her name. Sadie struggled to breathe and demanded to know who she was. The answer bent the air.

"They buried me to survive. You carried my blood back to me."

Lights flickered violently. The doll trembled, its glow intensifying, and Sadie screamed that it did not belong here. Laughter cracked through the room like thunder. The spirit said it belonged to the blood, to the roots, to the child who listened when the ground spoke. Desperation took over. Sadie tore the pendant from her neck and threw it toward the window, toward the oak outside, certain that if it touched the earth again it would end. The doll moved before it hit the ground, not fast, not far, just enough. Its porcelain fingers closed around the pendant, and every candle in the house flared to life at once.

The voice came again, calm and certain. Ending it was impossible. Sadie was already it. Wind tore through the open window, carrying the raw scent of freshly turned soil. Sadie collapsed to her knees, sobbing, and begged it to stop lying. The answer was gentle now, almost kind. She was told to look at her hands. Roots glowed beneath her skin, curling around her wrists and vanishing upward. The debt, the voice said, was paid in full.

Thunder shook the house. Sadie screamed and hurled the doll against the wall. It dissolved instead of breaking, splitting into dozens of glowing shards that hovered in the air, each one whispering her name as they rushed into her chest. Light poured through her, her back arching, her eyes burning gold as the hum rose into a roar that rattled the walls.

Then the storm ended.

Silence filled the room.

The mirror stood whole again. The doll was gone.

Sadie stood before the glass, breathing hard. Behind her reflection stood Thema, Bibi, Verna, and the faceless woman. Thema said Sadie had carried them all. Sadie asked what would happen now. The faceless woman stepped forward and said the debt had been claimed.

The mirror rippled.

Sadie's reflection changed.

The face staring back belonged to Thema.

Sadie tried to speak, but no sound came. The reflection smiled, not with comfort, but with certainty, and lifted its hand. Outside, the oak groaned as its roots tore deeper into the earth beneath the house, and the floor cracked beneath Sadie's feet.

Something inside her shifted.

Deep beneath the tree, something ancient answered.

Epilogue

The Whispering Field

Two years later

The town had changed in quiet ways that only time could manage. Paint peeled from old houses that once gleamed. The church bell rang less often, as if even it had grown tired. Storms came and went, leaving the air heavier than before, thick with the feeling that something had passed through and never fully left.

The oak tree remained. It stood tall in the backyard, wide and sprawling, its roots thick as bone beneath the soil. It had outlived every generation that feared it and every silence that tried to bury what it held.

Sadie sat beneath it with her knees drawn to her chest, a book resting open in her lap, though she had not turned a page in a long while. She was fifteen now. Taller. Quieter. Her beauty had sharpened with age and loss, and though her eyes still carried the warmth of gold and earth, they held something deeper now. Something that had watched grief arrive and learned how to survive it.

The doll was gone.

The house was quiet.

The voices were silent.

At least, that was what she told herself.

She had learned how to live with quiet again, or at least how to pretend she could. Each morning, she walked to the field beyond the church where Grandma Verna once hung laundry and let the wind do the work. The smell of grass and apples followed her there, familiar and persistent, like memory refusing to fade. Sometimes she noticed movement at the edge of her vision. A flash of white fabric. A glint of something smooth and pale. Each time she turned, there was only wind and tall grass bending low.

At night, her dreams returned to the same place. Roots stretched long and glowing beneath the soil, winding through darkness, pulsing faintly as if alive. They whispered in a language she almost understood, their message always the same.

The blood remembers.

Always.

Sadie had moved back into her grandmother's house. Her mother lived in the city now with new walls and quieter nights. She called when she could, her voice careful and loving, as if afraid to say the wrong thing.

They both knew the truth.

Sadie was not the same girl she had been.

The pendant hung on the wall now, locked behind glass beside Grandma Verna's photograph. Every so often, when the light struck it just right, it shimmered faintly with blue fire before going still again. Sadie told herself it was only a reflection, even though reflection had always meant something different in her family.

That afternoon, she sat by the window writing in a journal. It was not a diary. It was a record. She filled its pages with dreams, with moments she could not explain, with fragments of memory that did not feel like her own. Outside, the wind moved through the field in slow waves, brushing the tall grass like fingertips searching for something familiar. The sound made her pause. It was not the normal kind of wind.

It carried rhythm. Almost a hum. Sadie lifted her head and looked toward the oak. Its branches swayed gently while the rest of the trees stood still.

"I hear you," she whispered.

The sound faded.

Then came a knock at the door. Her breath caught. No one came here anymore. The knock sounded again, softer, patient. Sadie rose and crossed the room, her bare feet silent on the wooden floor. When she opened the door, no one stood there. Only a small envelope rested on the porch, pale and worn, tied with red thread. Her heart skipped as she bent to pick it up. The paper felt old in her hands, older than it should have been, and it carried the faint scent of lilacs and rain. Inside was a single folded note. The handwriting looped delicately across the page, graceful and familiar. The ink shimmered faintly, as though it had never dried.

She read it once.

Then again.

My dearest child,
The door you opened cannot be closed.
The blood you carry is not done speaking.
The story does not end with you.
It begins again with me.
Thema

Sadie's breath left her in a slow rush. The paper slipped from her fingers and drifted to the floor.

Outside, the oak tree moved once, though no wind stirred the air.

From somewhere inside the house, faint and unmistakable, came a sound she had not heard in two years.

The doll's hum... low, steady, and alive.

Sadie closed her eyes and whispered into the quiet, "I knew you'd come back."

The lamp flickered once.

Then the light went out.

www.ingramcontent.com/pod-product-compliance
Lightning Source LLC
LaVergne TN
LVHW050934080826
845145LV00004B/1258

* 9 7 8 1 9 6 1 2 1 3 2 9 6 *